VALLEY OF SECRETS

1995. Tammy Sands returns to her grandparents' home in Arcana Valley near Hebden Bridge. What happened to alienate her from her family? Before she can unravel the answers, she, and handsome detective Rick Turpin, find themselves immersed in a kidnapping, hidden treasures and the centuries-old battle between Tammy's family and the villainous Lord Nibberton. The young lovers must solve enigmatic riddles whilst fighting for their lives. Will the Valley reveal its supernatural secrets to Tammy and Rick in time?

ALAN C. WILLIAMS

VALLEY OF SECRETS

Complete and Unabridged

LINFORD
Leicester

First published in Great Britain in 2020

First Linford Edition
published 2021

A catalogue record for this book is available
from the British Library.

ISBN 978–1–4448–4678–2

Published by
Ulverscroft Limited
Anstey, Leicestershire

Set by Words & Graphics Ltd.
Anstey, Leicestershire
Printed and bound in Great Britain by
TJ Books Ltd., Padstow, Cornwall

This book is printed on acid-free paper

1

Secrets. We all have them. Everyone we ever knew. Everyone we *never* knew.

Looking at the overflowing boxes of paper, files and notebooks now stacked in my grandmother's lounge, I realised that places keep their secrets too. Dark, forbidden secrets. Concealed truths that were never meant to be revealed to others.

Now my aunt and I were sorting through them, I felt apprehensive about unearthing those family mysteries. And I wondered, would the questions I had about my own life be answered at last?

* * *

'Fancy a drink, Tammy?' Auntie Amanda yelled over the rain pounding on the windows.

I had visions of a cold pint of cider

1

but I knew that wasn't what she meant. It was only eleven in the morning. Too early . . . even for me.

'Yes, please,' I called back without enthusiasm, as I lifted yet another box of papers from the cupboard, almost choking on the dust that swirled around it. Removing my glasses to rub my aching eyes, I sat back on the velvet-covered settee.

Well, 1995 was shaping up to be another boring year in my life. Don't get me wrong, boring was a good thing these days. No fights between my parents or rows with my would-be boyfriend, Kyle. Also, my health problems hadn't been too bad for the past few weeks — although that usually was a sign of forthcoming days of payback.

Unfortunately, my quiet life away from other people was on hold again. I'd been asked to spend time assisting Auntie Amanda to clear out my grandparents' house in the middle of nowhere. Gramps had long since passed on, and Gran had moved into town.

Not that I had anything against Yorkshire, but this particular place in the Valley now seemed so isolated. I didn't like being away from the bustle of Manchester. Even the nearest town — with the exception of the chippy and pubs — closed at six.

I was a business consultant and worked by myself at home, using one of those newfangled computers. What outstanding tasks I did have, I'd brought with me to complete during the evenings.

I was well and truly cheesed off being here, though. It was bucketing down — cats and dogs. Judging from the sound, I'm certain that there were a few cows thrown in.

It wasn't as though I knew my grandparents well — or my aunt. We'd not seen one another for eleven years so I'd been surprised when Auntie Amanda had rung to ask for my help getting the house ready for sale. She said she'd had to call in a few favours to track me down, though I was certain I'd sent details of my latest address in my last, unanswered letter to Gran.

When I'd protested, she'd told me I was entitled to half the proceeds from the house sale so I'd better get my 'rear end' over here.

I'd been shocked. I'd thought Mum and I had been disinherited. After all, none of my letters had ever had a response.

Right now, opening yet another folder of junk in a creepy old house cut off from civilisation by a flooded road, I wondered if it was worth it. It didn't make up for the lack of family contact regardless of me constantly trying. I hadn't mentioned my anger, or the reason for it, as yet. But when I saw my gran, the first thing I'd ask her was why she'd abandoned me.

★ ★ ★

Amanda returned from the Seventies-style kitchen, carrying a tray with two black coffees plus a packet of custard creams . . . my favourites.

'Thought that would bring a smile to that sour puss,' my aunt said. I looked up as she sat down opposite me, placing the tray on a small table.

She was right. I'd been a right misery. I apologised before going to wash my hands. For all I knew, those boxes had been stored there since the war. The first one.

Removing my glasses again, I put them on the shelf under the partly silvered mirror. I preferred not to be reminded of my blemished skin any more than I had to.

As I returned to sit down, a folder fell onto the well-worn carpet. A bundle of envelopes spilled out, scattering from the red bow that had been used to tie them together.

'Great,' I said. 'A bit more mess.'

'Just leave them, Tammy. Relax. Besides, I want to have a chat; one that's long overdue.'

Here it comes, I thought.

5

I stared out of the window at the incessant downpour. Four days now. In spite of the overhead lights, it was dark in the room and even darker outside. The bushes and trees in the garden didn't help, overgrown to the point of unruliness.

At least I could munch while I listened, putting four biscuits on my plate and passing the rest across. Then I noticed my aunt was staring at a newspaper cutting lying on the floor.

'What is it?' I asked. Amanda bent down to retrieve the cutting as well as the pile of mail.

'This.' She passed it to me.

I read it and glanced at the grainy photo; some thirty-something guy on holiday.

'So, this Darren Bruce guy had gone missing, possibly kidnapped. No big deal.'

'No, read it properly. Use that clever brain of yours. What's wrong with this?'

I sat up straight, putting the half-eaten biscuit back on the plate. I'd just been given a compliment by someone I hardly knew. My memory had helped me through school and university when my illness had often made me bed-ridden.

The connection hit me immediately.

'He's from Uppermill . . . where you live, Aunt Amanda.' Uppermill in Saddleworth; population 4,478 at the last census. 'Did you know him?'

'No, but it was one of my last mis-per cases before I went on maternity leave. No joy, unfortunately.'

Ah — police jargon. 'Mis-per' must be missing persons.

'You're both from the same town. And Gran has some info about him. Coincidence.'

'A copper doesn't believe in coincidences and neither should you. What are the chances of my mum having a local newspaper article about a missing guy from the same town as me?'

'Since Uppermill is a fair old way from here, the chances are slim,' I confessed. 'But Gran was always a hoarder.'

I had pleasant memories of staying here years ago. Sometimes I wondered how much better my teenage years would have been staying with Gran and Gramps instead of my parents; people who never knew the meaning of affection.

'Maybe.' Amanda wasn't convinced.

I examined my aunt's face. She was a police officer, always searching out vague patterns and tying loose ends together. Me, I dealt in absolutes; facts and mathematics. I worked with one of those so-called think tanks. The pay was good but the fact that I could work from home was even better. I wasn't at ease being involved with other people and, despite my skills, I often felt so inadequate.

'What are you staring at, Tammy?'

I felt my cheeks going red. I dropped my gaze to my hands and the plate on my lap.

'You, Aunt Amanda. Sorry . . . I guess I'm envious. You seem so focused and strong. And you're pretty — even

8

with that messy hair.'

I surprised myself with my candour. Maybe I recalled how close we were once.

My aunt was smiling broadly. Then she burst out laughing. I didn't understand.

'Firstly, Tammy, can we drop the 'Auntie' bit? It makes me feel so ancient. I'm only thirteen years older than you. Secondly, you don't have to be envious of me. We're so much alike.'

Really? I began to grin. True, we both had blonde hair, but mine was long and wavy whereas Amanda's looked like a robin's nest, spiky bits sticking out everywhere except where they were supposed to. I wore a demure red dress with white trim. Amanda had a tattered blouse and holey, faded jeans. We were cheese and chalk.

As if reading my mind, she continued, 'Look past the appearances, love. Look underneath.'

I tried but the truth was, I didn't know my aunt. Not really. Maybe now

9

was the time to start building bridges.

I broke into one of my coughing fits.

'I bet you weren't bullied at school,' I eventually managed. The insults I endured had ranged from Smarty-Pants to colourful terms that would make a sailor blush. Being good at exams wasn't good for someone as insecure and screwed-up as me.

'Oh, I don't know about that, Tammy. Try going through primary school being called Amanda the Panda.' She smiled at the joke.

'I used to be called Panda too,' I confessed. 'I went overboard with eye make-up for a while, trying to disguise my sickly appearance. I guess I still use too much.'

It also made it easier to hide the damaged me inside, some teacher had once observed in an attempt to help me.

A flash of lightning chased by reverberations of thunder startled us. I jumped up and went to the larger window at the back of the house; the one that overlooked the verdant fields of the valley. Amanda joined me, clutching the bunch of letters.

Across the hills, the strobed flashes were now more frequent as renewed cascades streamed down the glass. The valley shimmered as if distorted, reminding me of the fun house mirrors on Blackpool's Pleasure Beach. Nothing outside looked real any longer.

The lights flickered and went out. I shuddered.

'Are you OK, Tammy?' Amanda's arm rested on my back. It felt good. My mother would never hug me, and as for my father . . . I rested my head on her shoulder.

'I loved the pitter-patter of rain on the roof when I slept here as a child. It was like a lullaby. Gran would bring hot chocolate, then sit on the bed telling stories or just listening as I read. I hated it when she and Mum had that fight . . . '

'Come on, love. Your coffee's getting cold,' said Amanda gently.

As we turned away from the window a shadow moved across it. I stopped.

'What is it?'

'Thought I saw someone outside. Probably my imagination. Who'd be out there in this weather?'

Just then the lights came back on. I heard the fridge start up too. We sat down and munched our biscuits in silence. I was lost in the past, surrounded by the floral wallpaper and carpets that were once a refuge in my traumatic childhood.

My mother and father were . . . well, the term today would be dysfunctional. Back then, I thought all parents were like them. There was no love between them . . . or me.

My grandparents had never taken to my father. Rightly so. He'd slowly and subtly taken away my mother's vibrancy and joy, crushing it to the point where she turned to alcohol. As for me, I was an inconvenience. It was easier to lock me in my room with a bunch of books than to spend any time loving me. They

were both dead now and I'd survived
. . . but not without some deep scars.

Was it too late to rebuild my life with
what was left of my relations? I
wondered. After all, my Auntie was
pregnant. It would be wonderful to be a
part of her future family. Her husband
was overseas at present. I'd never met
him — yet, from Amanda's comments,
he was a wonderful man.

To be honest, this place had mixed
memories for me. Wrapping some
colourfully striped glasses in newspaper
the previous day, I remembered them as
one of those childhood incidentals that
were a part of my growing-up. A
comforting, familiar part.

And yet . . . something bad had
happened to me just before that row. It
was so vague, I couldn't recall any
details. It was one of many questions I
intended to ask my gran . . . eventually.

Generations of our family had lived
here though. Gramps once told me they
were 'guardians', but that was when he
was ill and his mind was a bit lost.

Although I was only young back then, I thought it was a weird thing to say.

Amanda had broken the news to me that Gramps had died four years earlier. No one had contacted me at the time. When I mentioned this, she insisted they had. Another thing that didn't make sense.

I became aware of Amanda speaking to me.

'Earth to Tammy. Come in, Tammy.'

'Sorry. Miles away. I'm listening now.'

Amanda passed me the bundle of envelopes. She appeared agitated.

I opened the first letter, which had a typewritten address — my grandparents' PO Box.

Amanda explained that all the mail for the few inhabitants of the valley was delivered to boxes at the nearest Post Office, in Hebden Bridge. When I said that was odd, she suggested the postman was scared of coming to this part of the Dales.

The letter must have been sent a

while ago, judging by the stamp. Inside was a single sheet of paper with cut-out letters stuck to it.

'*Who's afraid of the big, bad wolf,*' I read out.

As if to emphasise the disturbing nature of the note, the lights flickered once more.

I tried to dismiss it. 'Obviously some nut-job with nothing better to do than send . . .'

Amanda interrupted. 'That's what I thought, but check out the postmarks.'

All but two of the six letters had dates that could be read. The earliest was nine years in the past, the last was just five months ago.

'Seems like a pretty dedicated person.'

'Hmmm. What do the others say?' I enquired.

'Some are nasty, others spooky. The second one says *Ring a ring a rosie.* You know, the nursery rhyme. I wonder why your gran kept them. They must mean something to her.'

Gran had left her beloved home as it

was too much for her to manage with her arthritis. She'd moved into Hebden a few weeks before. I hadn't summoned the courage to see her since I'd arrived. Too many memories and regrets, I told myself. The flooded track out of here made my excuses academic.

'Perhaps we should leave them for the moment. There are enough other things to sort out. No point trying to make sense of them if Gran can tell us what they're all about,' I suggested.

'Have we got a 'too difficult' box?' Amanda asked with a grin. In a corner of the room we had labelled cardboard boxes; red stickers for the charity shop, blue for recycling, green for the tip, yellow for Amanda's house in Uppermill and purple for my reasonably spacious two-bed flat in Manchester. Gran already had all she needed and wanted in her new accommodation.

'Hey. The rain's stopping.' I went to the window. 'I can see blue sky. The road might be passable soon. Our supplies are low — especially biscuits.'

'I wonder whose fault that is,' Amanda said. 'Why don't you go and check, Tammy? You could do with some fresh air.'

Sunlight flooded the room. My aunt was right. I had bad memories of being cooped up.

The pewter-grey clouds had vanished to wherever such clouds go. I sat on the chair by the front door to change my slippers for Doc Martens.

It was quite steamy out there. Droplets of rain were still falling from the trees onto the table and chairs under the huge mulberry tree. From the trees beyond came the sound of a cuckoo. We'd had great times here, Gramps on his tractor, Gran and me in her herb and veg garden.

'I wonder if my bridge is still there,' I muttered to no one in particular. It was a slight detour off the gravel road, and not far from where the road was prone to flooding as it swept past Misty River.

Gramps had painted a sign on the wooden structure during one visit when

I was nine. I was so pleased, and wanted to show my parents when they came to collect me. They'd ignored me. As far as I knew, they never did visit it. And then there was that big fight.

Even though the path through the garden was overgrown with weeds and long grass, it was easy enough to make my way to the stream. It, in turn, flowed into Misty River. I managed the brisk walk without getting my bare legs too wet.

Tammy's Bridge was still there, slightly the worse for wear with moss and lichen covering part of my neatly painted name. The gurgling brook was bubbling and eddying noisily as it surged over the stones and sand. Of all the places I'd lived, this farm was the one with the best memories.

Something was out of place, though. I spied it a dozen yards further on where the rivulet ran through the dappled shadows of a willow.

The bright blue wasn't natural. I edged across the bridge and along the bank, careful not to slip.

Was it some rubbish, washed down from the tree-clad hills surrounding the valley? Edging closer, I could see it was clothing. A jumper? It was difficult to tell with the mud and leaf litter.

I heard a rustle from the undergrowth — something large, judging by the crunch and squelch of broken twigs. Maybe a fox or deer?

I had to see what was by the creek. Feeling apprehensive, I edged closer before kneeling down to touch the blue coat. Shaking off the debris, I dunked it in the water to clean it before searching the zipped pockets for an indication of the owner's identity. My fingers found a plastic bag, knotted at the opening. I saw coins inside. Old ones, quite heavy. Could they be gold?

Curious, I riffled through the other pockets of the anorak and extracted a wallet.

Now we're getting somewhere.

The wallet was in good condition, seemingly protected by the tight seal of the special zipper.

There was a credit card inside. I examined the name, peering closely at it. My eyesight wasn't great at the moment.

Bruce, Darren, I read. Where had I heard that name before?

The missing person from Uppermill.

I stood, clasping the anorak and looking around to see if there was anything else amiss.

Oh, Lord, Gran. What on earth have you got yourself mixed up with?

2

The police didn't take long to arrive. It seemed Darren Bruce's disappearance was far more than a man just wandering off for a few days.

Amanda was there to support me. We had as many questions as the police about the connection between Darren's coat being here and my gran.

In addition, there were the coins. They were indeed gold, according to Amanda, and quite old. Valuable, too.

'No, I don't have a clue how it got there. Maybe washed downstream by the rain?' I repeated. 'And before you ask, I didn't kidnap him and I'm darn sure my grandmother didn't either.'

I was upset and angry and frightened, all at the same time. The young uniformed officer decided not to press it.

'Calm down, Tammy. He's just doing his job.'

There were two officers searching the house, wandering in and out of the front door. Most of the mud from their shoes had worn off before they reached the lounge; however the cream carpet was already in dire need of cleaning.

Amanda followed my gaze. She hugged me.

'Gran would have a fit. She was always very houseproud.'

'Now they probably think she has him hidden somewhere in a locked room.'

The coat appeared to have been recently lost, much more recently than the date its owner had last been seen.

Amanda had done her own check when I'd brought it back, while we waited for the local constabulary. She'd found a shop receipt from Hebden Bridge dated two days ago, tucked in one pocket. It looked as though someone had written a message on the reverse, yet the only discernible word was *'elp'*. The rest had been washed off.

'Oh, hell. Someone should tell Gran.'

That someone not being me . . . Suddenly that thought seemed so wrong. I should have made more of an effort to contact her, especially after Mum died. For some reason, I hadn't.

No way did I want police knocking on her door interrogating her before she found out what was happening, though.

'Already done,' Amanda said. 'She was more concerned about you than the situation, Tammy.'

I moved to the rear window that overlooked the valley. The house was situated well away from the only road which ran the length of the valley alongside Misty River. The goat and cows on the other side of the dry-stone wall were oblivious to the drama. I envied them.

At least the rain had stopped. The lush greenery and cotton wool clouds helped settle my agitated thoughts.

There was a brusque sound of footsteps on the hall tiles. Another copper, I assumed. A young, casually dressed guy with a bright orange tie, entered the room, spoke to the constable then marched over to Amanda and me.

'Detective Sergeant Turpin. Who found the coat?'

'I did. Tammy Jordan. Twenty-three years old. Freelance consultant. Aquarius. Size five shoe. And happily single,' was my curt reply.

I was tired and needed something proper to eat. Both DS Turpin and Amanda were staring at me in surprise.

'And you are?' the policeman asked my aunt.

'Amanda Lightfield.'

'And are you single too?' he asked sarcastically.

She gave him a withering stare as she patted her baby bump.

I decided to try and defuse the situation I'd caused. As patiently as possible, I explained why I was here and my relationship to the owner. Nonetheless, the tone of his questions indicated a total lack of compassion for my situation. I was becoming more irritated with this arrogant man. Policeman or not, I decided to respond with similar belligerence.

If he decided to arrest me at least I'd get fed. I was sure that's what they had to do in police stations. I'd seen it on *The Bill*, usually followed by the prisoner grabbing the dish of food and throwing it over the Custody Sergeant saying something like, 'I'm not eating this slop, you filthy pig.'

Somehow Amanda sensed my impending response so she interrupted.

'DS Turpin, is it? We have already given a statement to your colleagues. Your behaviour is out of order,' she stated confidently.

His cheeks flushed with anger. I actually thought his neatly trimmed chocolate hair was standing erect like that of a cat in a fight.

'I believe you continued the inspection of the coat after you'd realised the implication of discovering Mr Bruce's clothing. That's contaminating the evidence, you silly woman. Who do you think you are, anyway?'

This time it was Amanda who bristled.

'Actually, I know who I am, DS Turpin. I've known for quite a while. I'm an Inspector. Greater Manchester Constabulary. This house and land belong to my mother.'

That took him down a peg or two, momentarily.

'You have no jurisdiction here, Mrs Lightfield.'

Amanda gave a forced smile.

'True. Plus, I am on maternity leave in case you hadn't noticed. However, I am a ranking officer and politely request you address me as such.'

'My apologies, Inspector. You are correct. Yet you did contaminate the evidence by touching it without gloves.'

Amanda was becoming impatient.

'Although any forensic evidence would have been destroyed by the weather, I did wear gloves. What's

26

more, I bagged them in forensic evidence bags I carry with me and passed them onto the first officer on the scene. Here's his receipt.'

DS Turpin tried to maintain his stern demeanour. He examined the receipt officiously, recording details in his notebook.

Amanda turned away, then paused.

'DS Turpin, eh. Not Dick Turpin, by any chance? This 'silly 'woman' has heard your name mentioned even in Lancashire.'

The young man stepped back. I suddenly felt sorry for him.

'I . . . I prefer Rick, Inspector Lightfield. My apologies for that 'silly' remark and any disrespect to you and Miss Single . . . sorry, Miss Jordan. It's just that it's a very important case and I'm the senior officer. I came on a bit officious-like. Sorry.'

'Just a tad, Detective Sergeant.' She gazed out at more grey clouds arriving. 'It looks as though it's going to rain again. I assume you've checked for any more of Mr Bruce's possessions along the riverbank?'

It was a gentle prompt that did the trick. He'd clearly forgotten so he hurried off to follow my aunt's advice. Not before thanking her, though.

* * *

We watched him sprinting towards the bridge.

'He's quite fit,' I observed, then realised I'd said the wrong thing again. 'I mean, he must do a lot of exercise.'

'I know what you mean, Tammy. And you were right the first time.' My aunt doubled over. 'Going to sit down now, Tammy. Baby's complaining. Don't suppose you could make us a bite to eat? I have a feeling it'll be a long and stressful day.'

I fluffed some cushions up for her before scooting off to the kitchen. Seeing my aunt's steely gaze when dealing with the DS, I was glad she was here.

After preparing some food and pouring fruit juice, I returned to the lounge. Outside we could hear voices of police. The rain wasn't long in returning.

Finishing lunch first, I decided to read those letters properly. Clearly, they were written by a person known to my grandparents.

'Junior's kicking. Would you like to feel?' Amanda asked me. A little apprehensively, I placed my hand on her tummy.

'Oh. He's a strong one,' I exclaimed.

'Or she. Paul wants a girl. Me, I'm not bothered. What about yourself? Boyfriend? Plans to marry?'

'As if!' I laughed. My parents' fiasco of a marriage hadn't totally put me off the idea. 'I did have a guy who was interested in me but he was too demanding. Kyle Frederick Costello. Said his mates called him Rooster — because of the KFC connection, I guess. In retrospect he wasn't at all my type but he was persistent. Really weird.'

29

'Like a stalker?' My aunt was showing a concerned interest in me. It felt good.

'Not that bad. I ended up moving and haven't seen him again. That was five months ago.'

I turned my attention back to the letters; an interlude to take our minds off the activity outside. No doubt DS Turpin would return quickly enough.

The letters had been bound with a red satin ribbon. Amanda had arranged them in date order. The latest was on top with a franking date of March, 1995, just three months ago. They were all posted at Hebden, and had the same stamp denomination; twenty-two pence.

'You've noticed something, Tammy?'

'Maybe. You'll probably think I'm one of those people who are obsessed with stamps but I'm not. I simply remember things. Mostly useless facts. This stamp is of the Lady of the Lake and came out in 1985 as part of the Arthurian Collection. Does knowing that make me a geek?'

'Yes. But 'geek' is good these days, or so I hear.' Amanda gave me a wan smile. 'Anything else hidden in that super brain of yours?'

'First class stamps were seventeen or eighteen pence back then. Seems strange to use a higher denomination than was needed. Also, to use the same stamp over all those years? See where they used two stamps when the price went up above twenty-two pence four years ago.'

'Barking mad, but law-abiding. Why use the same stamp, Tammy?'

I considered that. The most obvious answer was the most logical.

'Guess they bought a lot of them back in 1985 and don't send many letters.'

Amanda heaved herself up and wandered over to the front window.

'There are quite a few vehicles out there now. I can see them through the trees. Between you and me, this inquiry is high priority. Missing children are the only other major incident to get this sort of response.'

She looked over at me, but said nothing about what had happened when I'd last been here. Some things were better left for the present time.

'Letters?' I suggested again. She returned, bringing a pen and notebook with her.

As she sat next to me, I remembered. 'Do we need gloves? Fingerprints and all that?'

'Don't think it matters, Tammy. There's nothing that suggests criminal activity or any real connection to Darren Bruce's coat. If you want, I could grab some more Marigolds from the kitchen but seriously . . . doing this? There's probably a simple explanation. You read the messages. I'll record the content and date. You always did like to play detective.'

I'd forgotten that. I took out each paper with its glued-on letters and read them out to Amanda.

Suddenly, I stopped. I must have

missed the significance of one on my first read through.

'Amanda. Maybe there is a connection between that coat and the letters. Listen to this one. In an envelope dated 1998.

'*Gold coins, silver coins, shiny jewels and treasure. Hidden by the church men, discovered at my leisure.* What do you make of that?'

Amanda sat up. She was suddenly quite interested. 'Did you say 'church men'?'

'Yeah. Exactly who is this Darren Bruce and why the intense interest in him? I'm not that naïve, Amanda. There's no way an inspector would be involved in a normal mis-per case. Now there are at least five police out there, including Supercop. For what? An investigation of some guy's anorak?'

'You're a perceptive young lady, Tammy Jordan. What I'm going to tell you is not something I want broadcast. Dick Turpin might know a bit but the others . . . well, keep it to yourself. OK?'

'OK. I don't have anyone to share it with anyway, Amanda. Not many friends or family, especially these days.'

'Well, Darren is a special investigator with the government. His disappearance, hot on the heels of a report that he was onto some discoveries in this area, has prompted a clandestine investigation by a select few in the police force. I was, and despite being pregnant, still am, one of those officers trying to discover what happened to him. You suggested before that my mother having a newspaper cutting of his disappearance wasn't a coincidence. You were right.'

'Let me guess. He was on the trail of some religious treasure hoard from around the early 1500s?'

My aunt turned quickly, her eyes wide.

'How could you possibly . . . ?'

'Not that difficult, Amanda. The coins had Henry Vll's inscription on

34

them. He was king from 1485 to 1509. Can I assume that the treasure was hidden during the time of the Suppression of the Monasteries?' I pushed my glasses up to the bridge of my nose and scratched my ever-itchy arm. 'Henry VIII founded the Church of England and 'acquired' the funds held by the newly banned Catholic Church to fill his own coffers.'

'I'm impressed, Tammy. I want you on my pub quiz team next time we have one. That's one impressive memory you have there.'

'Thanks,' I replied, self-consciously pulling my sleeve down to hide my blemished arm. It was a novelty to receive a compliment from a family member.

Now, we had a connection between the coat and Gran's enigmatic letters. The question was simply, what did it all mean?

I re-tied the ribbon around the envelopes and snuggled in next to Amanda. A whiff of perfume wafted over from her.

'Don't tell me you still wear LouLou? It's so Seventies!'

'Matches my flares and disco dresses,' she joked back. We studied the puzzling list that had begun in 1987.

Remember the promise, Mildred Hathaway.

Gold coins, silver coins, shiny jewels and treasure. Hidden by the church men, discovered at my leisure.

Ring a ring a rosie.

When 'tis silin', off bleggin', eyen the goosegogs, thissen.

Today's the day Teddy has his picnic.

Who's afraid of the big, bad wolf? Vervain won't save her now.

'Well? Any clues that you can see, Detective Tammy? Because it's clear as mud to me,' Amanda confessed.

'They clearly meant something to Gran.'

'Tammy. Mum keeps things. Yesterday I found three books of Green Shield stamps in a drawer. Even so, the way she fastened these together suggests there was a message in them.'

36

I racked my brain. Some of the references were known to me, yet putting them together into a coherent solution was out of my reach.

'Vervain is a medicinal herb. But the rest . . . ?'

My thoughts were interrupted by the sound of the front door being opened and closed. There were two lots of footsteps. More police?

'OK to come in, ladies?' The voice was higher than DS Turpin's. A lot higher.

'Certainly, Kim,' Amanda answered.

Our new visitor, a short, dark-haired woman with glasses, entered confidently. The young Detective Sergeant followed her in.

'Amanda,' she said as she shook hands with my aunt. 'And this must be young Tammy, all grown up.'

I looked at her blankly.

'Detective Inspector Kim Byrne. Call me Kim; old friends and all that.' I assumed she'd been called in from a day off. Kim was dressed in trainers and a grey track suit with pink stripes. Her make-up and short bob were meticulous, though. Like her body language, it made a definite statement. *Don't let my petite stature fool you. I'm one tough woman.*

Kim turned to her subordinate. 'Coffee. Black. No sugar. Anything for you two?'

DS Turpin looked shocked. He'd probably never been ordered to make a drink by a woman before. I decided to assist him. The fact that he was good-looking had nothing to do with it.

'I'd best help,' I said. 'Temperamental kettle.'

I walked out into the hall, passing Rick who was still standing there like a stunned mullet. The simile was wrong, I decided. Mullets don't stand.

I grabbed his hand. 'Come on, DS Turpin.'

His hand was cold and wet — a bit like the rest of him, I imagined. It was technically summer but the rain had been falling from time to time, sometimes heavily. His hair was soaking.

'Looks like you could do with a hot drink too,' I commented as I switched the jug on. There was no problem with it. Grabbing a towel from a drawer, I offered it to Rick. He accepted it gladly, our hands brushing as he did so.

Unfortunately, I had to pull away, grabbing a tissue from my pocket to cough into. Damn and double damn. So much for that hint of romance. Not that any half-decent man would fancy me.

Regaining my composure, I said, 'You've not worked with her before?'

'No. I'm new to Calder Valley Division, though I grew up near here. Sickness and cutbacks meant no DIs were available so they brought her in from Halifax. From what I've seen, she lives up to her nickname.'

'Which is?' I raised my eyebrows enquiringly.

'I've said too much, Miss Jordan. Let's just make the drinks and get back.'

From the back of my mind, I recalled

vague images of long ago — the last time I'd been here at Gran's home. There was a younger version of the policewoman, kneeling down to hug me as I cried.

'Is it Bulldog Byrne? Once she has her teeth in some case, she never lets go?'

From the plain-clothes officer's expression, I was right.

We returned to the two women who were obviously catching up.

'The jacket and wallet have been confirmed as belonging to Darren Bruce by his wife,' she said for my benefit. 'The credit card too, last used by Mr Bruce the day prior to his disappearance, in the Post Office at Hebden. As for that till receipt with the message on it, that's still being tested.

'There was one thing though which you might not have noticed, Amanda. Or Tammy. Something very *X Files*-ish. Some powdery stuff on the wallet and coat that glows in the dark.

'Mrs Bruce was certain that her

husband had other items in the wallet like a family photo, yet there was no sign of those. I suspect our mis-per is being held somewhere and used the personal items to grab our attention. That means he's alive and being held somewhere further up the Valley.'

It was a concise update. Kim took a long sip of her drink.

'Why further up the Valley?' DS Turpin asked.

I blurted out the answer which was obvious to me. 'Because the stream starts up there and flows down to Misty River. If it had ended up there, it would have been much harder to pinpoint where the jacket was thrown in. Am I right?'

Saying that much led to another coughing fit. I excused myself.

'Excellent deduction, Tammy. Might I ask if you're OK? You look sickly.' Kim's concern echoed that she had shown me long ago.

'It's nothing new. I'm always having problems. Thanks for asking. What about the coins? Early 1500s? Gold?'

Kim smiled. 'I see you haven't lost that knack for recalling facts and figures. You were a right little know-it-all when I last saw you. I think you were learning that made-up language, Esperanto.'

'Yeah. I learned it. No use, though. No one else speaks it.' Trust me to be the world's ultimate nerd, I thought.

Another officer came in at the front door, then left immediately. That caused a gust of wind to blow our letter list from the coffee table. Kim put her cup down to retrieve the paper.

'What's this? *Ring a ring a rosie?*'

My aunt explained before concluding, 'Obviously some prankster enjoyed sending riddles to my parents.'

Kim studied the list intently.

'Maybe. Maybe not. Amanda, you should ask your mum if she can shed any light on them. There is something about that *Ring a ring a rosie* rhyme. Something sinister.'

I thought it very odd for her not to

mention the treasure and coin letter. Did she not want her subordinate to be aware of the connection?

Kim eyed the envelopes before facing me.

'Tammy. I want you to walk me through this morning's discovery of our jacket. I'd like an idea of what you saw and did, especially this figure you noticed around the house. Do you feel up to it?'

Amanda put a comforting hand on my shoulder.

'I'll come with you.'

I was grateful for that. Kim appeared compassionate enough yet, despite my veiled recollection, I didn't feel I knew her at all.

'Let's go, then,' I said, getting to my feet.

Outside steam was rising from the wet ground as the sun again broke through the clouds. This time the stroll to my bridge wasn't as relaxing. The overgrown roses in the raised beds almost seemed to be reaching out to warn me against going. Yet what else could possibly be down there to cause me any more distress? Even the breeze's whispers sounded foreboding.

Reaching the rivulet, it was in full flow. Churning waters splashed my boots. Some figures were by the temporary tent placed over the discovery site. All the time I was answering Kim's detailed questions while other hushed voices seemed to be speaking in unison from all around.

'Are you OK, Tammy?'

'Yes. Fine.' There was no possibility I was admitting to auditory hallucinations! Kim was peering into a coppice of trees by the rivulet edge. Had she sensed the voices too?

'Sherwood Forest,' I commented to her unspoken question. I used to play in there.

Kim made her way across to the mixture of trees; chestnuts, rowan, ash and hawthorn clustered around the tree I used to call Old Man Oak. And there were the remnants of an ancient stone building hidden in the undergrowth

She ambled across the sparse grass and undergrowth, kneeling to examine the debris from the old rock wall more closely.

'So?' I asked.

'That rhyme. *Ring a ring of rosies, a pocket full of posies. A-tishoo. a-tishoo, we all fall down.*'

'That's one version of the poem,' she continued as she scrutinised the area. 'It's thought to be about the Bubonic or Black Plague. The 'roses' were a rash on the body, posies of flowers were carried to cover the smell of dead bodies, sneezing was a symptom and 'We all fall down' was death.'

Kim took her police radio from her bag.

Amanda commented, without thinking, 'No use. It's a dead zone here.'

Kim sighed at her inert radio and looked up.

'Exactly — but not the type you mean, Amanda. Looks like the remnants of some sort of memorial to those

45

that died in the plague here. Latin inscription on the stones.'

Walking towards her car, the radio eventually spluttered into life. She called headquarters and requested dogs and more officers to search upstream for any other signs of the missing man.

No sooner had she signed off than Amanda's mobile in her trouser pocket buzzed noisily.

My aunt answered. 'Slow down, Mum. You what? Wait . . . Put the officer on.'

As she waited, she turned angrily to Kim and Rick.

'Two uniform are there to arrest my mother. Is this your doing?'

The officers regarded one another in shock before Kim assumed control.

'Pass me your phone, Amanda. Please.' A few more seconds' pause. 'Hello. This is Detective Inspector Byrne. Who am I speaking to? . . . Listen to me, Constable. You will release Mrs Hathaway immediately, apologise profusely and wait for me to arrive. And if you don't believe who I am, then I suggest you contact your commanding officer and tell him that Bulldog Byrne is not a happy doggie.' The last sentence was quiet yet forceful. It scared me — and I wasn't the one in trouble.

'Sorry about that, Amanda, Tammy. There's been an anonymous phone call saying Mrs Hathaway had kidnapped someone. The police were told a man's bloodstained attaché case was in her car. When the officers did a search, it was there, hidden away. Moreover, they discovered whose it was when they checked the contents.'

'Who was the owner?' Amanda enquired. 'No. Let me guess. Darren Bruce.'

'How did you know?' said Kim.

'Someone's playing a chess game with us, Kim. And I'm getting quite angry at being pushed around like some pawn.'

3

Despite having nothing to do with my grandmother for so long, I couldn't believe what I'd heard. There was simply no possibility that she could be responsible.

This was a deliberate move by some local, designed to deflect the proper investigation.

'You two coming?' Kim said as she opened her car door. 'You as well, DS Turpin. You're my bag man. No need to thank me.'

The look on the young officer's face didn't suggest gratitude. However he assumed his new responsibilities graciously.

'Directions, please?' he asked Amanda.

'She's near Hebden. Do you know the way there, Detective Sergeant?'

'Like yours, Inspector, my family have lived in this valley for generations.

Now, if someone would pass me her keys, we'll get started.'

Kim handed the keys over with a sideways glance. 'I see we're going to make a good team, DS Turpin,' she said. 'Either that or you'll be back in uniform and on point duty for the foreseeable.'

As we headed off, I felt guilty about the past. Meeting up with my gran after all this time would be difficult enough. Adding a kidnapping to the equation would only make it worse. But what choice did I have? Whatever had happened between us, she needed me now.

★ ★ ★

It took around ten minutes to arrive at my gran's new home. She was in a detached two-bedroom bungalow on a secure estate for older people. The small private garden where she could indulge her insatiable love of growing plants was, according to Amanda, her favourite place.

Over the years I'd written to my grandparents a number of times, never receiving any reply. Whether it had been some sort of family dispute with my mum or not, I'd accepted that I wasn't welcome as a part of her family. Even so, I had persevered right up to this year.

That was until Amanda had contacted me on my unlisted phone number, saying that I'd always been a part of the family. None of it made any sense. Apparently, Gran had sent letters to me as well as me writing to her yet we'd never received one another's mail.

'You all right?' Amanda asked when we got out of the car. 'You're shaking like a leaf.'

I lifted my head. A part of me didn't want to see her. Not like this.

'Apprehensive. And on top of this police drama, meeting Gran again . . . it's going to be stressful, especially for her. She probably wouldn't recognise me if she saw me in the street. I wonder if she'll approve of who I've become.'

My aunt put her arm around my shoulder as she guided me to the front door.

'You're family. Of course, she'll love you. Priority is to sort out this mess first. Right, Kim?'

The door was opened by a youthful police officer. Gran was behind him. She smiled. Our fellow visitors identified themselves, showing their warrant cards.

Kim spoke up, taking Gran's frail hands in hers.

'I'm sorry you've been subjected to this, Mrs Hathaway. We're all here to sort out this situation, Amanda and your granddaughter Tammy too.'

Gran adjusted her glasses, as did I. She chose to address Kim first as she shuffled back to her lounge where we all sat at her invitation, me by her side.

'I remember you, officer, from when Tammy went missing.' She then turned to me, gazing at me fondly as she touched my cheek. 'You've grown a lot, young lady, my Tammy. Champion, if you don't mind me saying. I thought I'd never see you again.'

I reached over to give her a hug and kiss. The questions about what I'd just heard could wait. Right now, Gran needed me to just be there.

I sat down holding Gran's delicate hand. Kim chose a gentle approach, defusing the tension precipitated by the other police arriving earlier.

'Could I suggest a drink for you, Mrs Hathaway? A sweet tea always helps. Not so good for the figure but, in moderation, I find it works wonders.'

DS Rick was off once again to the kitchen. He went more willingly this time, understanding the value of putting victims at ease. My gran was plainly a victim of some malicious phone call.

It wasn't only Kim's tranquil, almost lullaby voice that was soothing us. It was her touch, her attention to my gran — and her interest in the keepsakes she had surrounded herself with in this, her special sanctuary.

Kim strolled around, examining photos in frames on the mantel and on the wall. She engaged my grandmother with questions about them while Amanda and I watched protectively. We needn't have worried. By the time Rick returned, they were like old friends.

Succinctly, Kim explained about the jacket that had been found, probing to see if Gran had any information which might help.

'Can you tell me whose coat it was that was found, Kim? I know all of the thirty or so families in Valley; some better than others. Some wassocks I wish I never met at all.'

Kim answered. 'A missing man called Darren Bruce. We believe he's been — '

'Abducted. Yes. I read that in the newspaper. From Uppermill, if I recall. I believe I met him some months ago — he visited me at the old house.'

The two policewomen exchanged glances.

'You met him? Are you sure, Mum?'

Amanda enquired, her hand resting on her mother's arm.

'I'm pretty certain. Do you have a colour photo? The one in the newspaper was very indistinct.'

Kim reached into her handbag then showed the photo to Gran. She let go of my hand to don her reading glasses before rubbing some pungent smelling cream onto her hands.

'Green mussel oil . . . helps with the arthritis. Now let's see that photo, please.'

We waited expectantly as she took her time, moving the photo in and out to focus better. Eventually, she spoke.

'Yes, that's him. The green eyes. Said he wondered if I had some old records he was researching. Pleasant youngster. Two kiddies, he has, both girls.'

She paused, still grasping the picture.

This whole scenario was becoming so much more mysterious than *The Bill*. Somehow, I reckoned it would take a lot more than a half hour, including commercials, to solve this crime.

I noticed that Rick had moved to the far end of the room and was on the radio, no doubt conversing with officers back at Calder Valley HQ.

'He wanted historical facts to do with the Valley, I gather. Although he didn't go into details, he was following up on summat from old documents from the Middle Ages and wondered if our family had our own records, especially from the time they were building the canals. Our ancestor, Eugene Hathaway, was mayor way back when.

'Anyhow, this Darren laddie asked me to see what I might find, saying he'd come back. He never did. Would have been a wasted journey.'

'Why's that, Gran?' I asked.

'I couldn't find owt he was interested in. Mind you, my filing system ain't what it should be. I tend to keep the odd bit of tutty.'

Amanda laughed. 'We've discovered that, Mum.'

'Oh, I don't know. Your dad's collection of Matchbox cars might be a fine gift for that bairn you're carrying, Amanda. Assuming it's a lad, of course. If not, there's your Sindy doll, her horse and her yellow car.'

To her credit, Kim hadn't pushed her investigative questions, allowing Amanda and Gran to chat. However she chose now to step in.

'Could you tell us anything more about Darren, please, Mrs Hathaway? What he'd discovered already, for example?'

Gran concentrated, smiling wistfully at me as she did so.

'I recall his calling card. It said he was from the Home Office. Oh aye. He was allus scratching at a rash on his neck. It was like the Fairy Touch but different, somehow.'

I sat forward, my heart rate increasing as my throat went dry. Gran noted my inquiring stance.

'A skin problem your gramps and I had years ago. Cerise spots.'

I rolled up the sleeve of my blouse.

'Like this, Gran?'

Gran appeared shocked. 'Dear Lord, child. What are they still doing there? The cream should have cleared that up long since.' She peered into my face. 'The nagging cough . . . the jaundice in your eyes. No wonder you're unwell, Tammy. You've still infected.'

I pulled away abruptly. Not the best thing to tell someone. Subconsciously I felt the two police and my aunt move away, ever so slightly.

'Infected?' said Amanda. 'Is it . . . contagious?'

'Not now. And I can cure her. I have some cream I used for such cases in the Valley. See the shape of the spots? The pattern they form?'

I peered at my arm closely. Amazingly, there was a pattern. Funny. I'd never noticed it before.

'They look like miniature flowers. Roses.'

Kim was intrigued. 'Excuse me, Mrs Hathaway. You mentioned that Darren had a similar rash . . . the Fairy Touch? But you said it was a different colour. What was it?'

57

'Blue. Rich . . . like gentian blue.' Gran pointed to a violet-blue flowering plant growing on the windowsill.

'Is there any chance he might be contagious?' Kim asked, concerned. After all her team were examining Darren's possessions.

'I doubt it,' Gran replied. 'Mind, the Fairy Touch can be spread though it's never fatal. Just makes you sickly, like.' She peered at me again. There was guilt on her aged-lined features.

Kim turned to ask Rick to contact her team but, efficient as always, he was already speaking on the radio. I heard him mention 'locking down the site and personnel' until they had a clearer idea of what they were dealing with.

'Could you please tell me more about this Fairy Touch, Mrs Hathaway?' Kim pressed her gently.

Gran laughed, in spite of the situation. I imagined that thinking of the term had triggered some memories of long ago.

'That was the name Miriam came up

with. Miriam Laws. She was the youngest of our group. I guess she called it that, 'cause of all that talk of fairies up in Cottingley around then.'

Kim turned to me, questioningly. It seemed I was already recognised as the resident expert on all things strange and downright useless.

I told them what I knew from my reading.

'Cottingley Fairies. Cottingley's a town up near Bradford. It's famous because of some black and white photos taken by two young girls in 1918, showing them playing with fairies near a stream. Caused quite a storm. Even Sir Arthur Conan Doyle believed they were real.'

Kim seemed to take a moment to process that. Most people hereabouts would be familiar with the belief in magical fae that pervaded children's literature when my gran was a child.

'Please continue, Mrs Hathaway. Did all your childhood friends have this skin complaint?'

'Most folk in the Valley have had it at one time or another. Sad to say it all began with one of our childhood adventures. We children caught it, then it spread. Manky, it was. Fortunately, my mother came up with a cream . . . a poultice that would clear it in days.'

This time it was Rick who spoke up.

'Are you saying your mother was like the wise woman of the valley, dispensing medicines? Made from what?'

'Plants of course, lad. Haven't you ever been stung by a nettle?' Rick nodded. 'And what do you put on it?'

'Dock leaves, of course. They counteract the poison on your skin.'

My gran grinned. 'I rest my case. My mum was a herbalist and taught me her skills; Valerian helps sleeping, passion flower for anxiety. And I have a special poultice that will rid you of that Fairy Touch, Tammy. From the look of you, it's long overdue. Itches like hell, doesn't it?'

I agreed. Nothing had reduced the

problem, not even steroid creams. That's why I kept my nails short.

Kim moved on. 'Do you believe that this Fairy Touch might be associated with Darren's abduction, Mrs Hathaway?'

'I do. Darren said his affliction was a sign he was getting reight close to his goal . . . whatever that was. Something important. It was in Arcana Valley too. That much he was certain about.'

I must have gasped as everyone turned to me.

Rick asked, 'Is that what its proper name is? I've grown up close to here. Everyone round abouts calls it Spooky Valley because of the disappearances and strange happenings.'

I recovered from the shock of hearing the word. Had Gran forgotten? I stared at her, willing her not to say anything before I explained.

'Arcana actually is Latin for 'mysterious' or 'secret'. 'Spooky' would be an accurate translation too.' Suddenly I felt sicker than ever. I had no idea that the connection between me and the Valley was this strong.

'You speak Latin, Miss Jordan?' Kim enquired. 'There aren't many of us around any longer.'

'No. But know the meaning of the word Arcana.' I glanced at Gran. 'It's my middle name.'

Kim stood, considering all that had been said.

'Great. We have one missing man, probably abducted, an infection which may or may not be dangerous and talk of fairies and magic potions; all in a place my supposedly educated DS calls Spooky Valley. What's more, Tammy here has her own connection to the Valley. Can it get any worse?'

As if on cue, like a scene from some television show, Rick's radio made a loud sound. He walked from the room to answer it, his muffled voice indicating some distress on his part. We waited expectantly.

When he returned his face was grim and he was noticeably upset.

'What is it, Rick?' I asked, in retrospect being a smidgen overly familiar.

'DI Byrne. You were correct about checking upstream, ma'am. There was a car dumped off the beaten track. It belongs to our mis-per. There were signs of violence inside.'

DI Kim Byrne summed it up for all of us.

'It would seem that Arcana Valley has more secrets than we ever could have expected.'

4

That wasn't all that Rick had to report. 'Miss Jordan mentioned she believed there was an intruder near the house when it was raining earlier. I asked forensics to check for indications and they reported back that footprints were found in the mud. Fresh.

And they appear to have been made by a woman, judging by the size. An unusual brand of boots called Hob-Nobs. I have to ask . . . '

Amanda and I shrugged simultaneously.

'Hob-Nobs? Sounds more like a biscuit, Rick.'

That reminded me. There was one biscuit left on the plate. I checked if anyone wanted it, before commandeering it.

Kim had her own question for Gran.

'Mrs Hathaway? If you had met this

missing man, could you tell me why you didn't contact the police when you read about his abduction? Amanda tells me you had a copy of the newspaper report.'

Gran looked at Kim with surprise in her gently wrinkled eyes.

'I did, Kim. I rang the same day. Hebden Bridge Police Station. I gave my details to a nice young man there but heard nowt since. At the time, I thought you weren't bothered. Now I can see that I should have persisted. This Darren person . . . he must be important.'

Rick was already on his radio again, reporting back that there was no record of any call.

'Are you certain you phoned, Mrs Hathaway?' he began. 'The mind can — '

'Young man,' my gran retorted angrily. 'I might be old but I do remember that. Check my phone records if you don't believe me.'

'Do it, Detective Sergeant. If your

station officer is screwing things up, I want to know.' Kim was fully in control.

Moments later a very sheepish Rick Turpin admitted that my gran had rung the station on the date she had claimed. The call had lasted almost fifteen minutes.

'Looks like a visit to your office is on the cards, DS Turpin. Someone there has slipped up big time. In the meantime, there are a few more things I'd like to hear about Mr Bruce, Mrs Hathaway. That is, if you feel up to it?'

'Anything I can do to help that poor young lad get back to his family, Kim. Ask away.'

* * *

After what felt like a few hundred questions and responses, the two detectives announced they were leaving.

Inquiries about the bizarre letters were never made; there were too many more pressing issues, I assumed. No doubt Kim would follow up on them, just as Amanda and I intended to.

Strangely, in a day filled with intrigue and drama, there was never any suggestion that any of us were suspects. Perhaps Kim knew something she wasn't disclosing, or maybe she accepted Gran was too old and frail to be a kidnapper.

I hadn't been on the scene until a few days ago, and as for Amanda? Well, she was police and would have more sense than to involve her own family.

No. I guessed the main suspect was the person who'd implicated my grandmother in the crime by planting evidence. In future, my gran wouldn't be leaving her car unlocked, I was sure about that.

When the others left, I chose to stay with Gran. It was her idea. 'Catch-up time,' she explained.

Amanda said she'd happily return to collect me in a few hours. I had plans to finish off some consultancy work, so I could post it tomorrow.

Finally, it was just my grandmother

and me, alone together for the first time in eleven years.

'Right, Miss Tammy. I realise you've got your own questions to ask, but first things first. Let's rid you of your Fairy Touch, once and for all.'

'If only you could, Gran.' I stared at the infection on my arm, wondering what it would feel like to be rid of the blight. 'If you could sort this out, I could kiss you.'

'Might take days, might take months, sweetheart. Why don't we just have a hug on account, lass? It would make this old lady's heart reight chuffed.'

Although awkward at first, I was soon sobbing with joy as we embraced. Those worries that my gran didn't love me disappeared immediately.

Eventually I pulled away, removing my glasses to wipe my eyes and sniffling.

'I love you so much, Gran.'

'And you too, Tammy. Give us a proper gander at that arm of yours, young'un. I need to formulate me a treatment plan.'

She examined the rash closely with a magnifying glass, ceasing only to jot down some notation or scribble it out with a muttered tut-tut. As she did so, I stared at her still luxuriant, neatly brushed hair. The smell of that green mussel oil was medicinal, almost hypnotic. Behind her, I noticed the same clock that had chimed each hour in those halcyon days I'd stayed in the Valley as a child. The mahogany wood and brass fitments shone in the afternoon sunshine. I heard Gramps' voice again, in my mind.

It's my clock, Tammy. Named after me — reight special, like.

When I'd asked him to explain, he'd said it was called a grandfather clock. Then he'd grinned and twirled his funny moustache with his fingers.

'Would you like me to wind the clock and set it to the right time?' I asked Gran, noticing the stilled pendulum.

'Clock's not worked since he passed, lass. It was his job to wind it. I prefer to keep it that way. Like a part of him is still with me. You understand, don't you, Tammy?'

'Yeah. Pleasant memories,' I agreed. 'I'm sorry for what's happened between us.'

There was a pause. The redness on my arm was itching more — almost as if it knew its days were numbered and was afraid.

'Gran. Quite a few doctors and dermatologists have tried to cure me. What makes you believe you can succeed?'

With swollen, knobbled fingers that were difficult to bend, Gran tapped her forehead.

'Practice, duck. My old mum and I, we studied the Touch for years. It's only found in the Dale.'

Another Valley puzzle, I realised.

'Come on, lass. Firstly, to my garden then to my lab.'

Disregarding the obvious pain from her arthritis, she took my hand. We made our way through the spick-and-span kitchen and out of the heavy door.

I'd expected lettuces and tomatoes but was amazed to see hundreds of labelled pots and bedded plants arranged in neat sectors.

'My medicine cabinet, young Tammy. We've got us a big task ahead. That rash of yours isn't only on that skin. The Touch burrows down inside you like rabbits digging a warren. It's affected you everywhere, hiding from them antibiotics and antivirals. Eleven years of the Touch will need a multi-pronged attack to clear it all out.

'Could you collect the ones I point out, lass? Just pop them on that tray yonder.'

There were some incredible names like Marsingorter and Flup-flup, though I recognised quite a few names on the plants, even one from the mysterious letters.

'Goosegogs? What are they, Gran?'

She stared as if I'd asked how to spell 'cat'.

'Everyone knows that, girl. Gooseberries. Honestly, I despair of you young 'uns. What do they teach you in schools these days?'

Then she gave me a wink.

Once we'd collected a dozen or so herbs, we returned to enter the second bedroom. She called it her lab. I could see why. Mortars and pestles, conical flasks, an electric centrifuge and distillation kit were all set up. Also there were labelled jars, some yellow with age with coloured powders or dried leaves. In one corner there was a largish plant growing happily away. The ice lolly stick poked into the soil read *Doris*.

'Is that . . . ?' I asked, recognising the distinctive leaf profile and the hint of an odour in the air which reminded me of university parties. Not that I'd gone to many.

Gran interrupted me. 'Doris is my favourite pot plant.' I smiled with her slight emphasis on the word 'pot'. 'Doris and me, we're old friends. And I'd 'preciate it if you don't mention her to Amanda or that Kim woman.'

I agreed. It seemed like my gran

wasn't the staid old pensioner I'd expected after all. She set to work on a magic potion consisting of Hamamelis (witch hazel), bear's claw, Prumenin and a number of other liquids and powders, rubbing the resulting mixture on her own arm. After giving it a sniff, she asked me to weigh out some bright green Myxticsia crystals that stank like rotten eggs. With great care, she added those to the crucible. Then she took out a blob of the bubbling gunge and took my arm to hold it out.

'Blinking heck, Gran. If you expect to put that on my arm — '

She stared into my eyes. 'Trust me, child.'

Talk about the cure being worse than the disease. If I had to spread this disgusting-smelling concoction on my skin every day, my love life was doomed to go from almost non-existent to being celibate forever.

'OK. Do it,' I said, gritting my teeth.

She dropped it on. Instead of heat, there was a sudden chill. I was amazed.

'Endothermic reaction. Takes the heat from your arm to evaporate the volatile chemicals. Now sniff.'

Warily I held it up towards my nose.

'Pineapple? I can live with that.'

The itch had ceased. My gran was a miracle worker. Either that, or a white witch. Either way, I felt better than I had in years. The rash had faded already. I hugged her for ever so long.

'That was the first dose. Extra strong. You won't require the Myxticsia from now on. No more smelly eggs. You'll need to apply it twice a day for two weeks. The red spots should vanish in a day or two — though don't let that make you complacent, like. The Touch'll be pretending it's gone. It's sneaky like that.'

She continued to ply me with potions and sprays designed to rid me of the cough and general malaise. By the time she'd completed her ministrations and taught me what to take and when, my head was spinning like a carousel.

'Valerian to sleep tonight, but don't

overdo it. I want you up and about tomorrow. It'll give that pretty body of yours time to mend overnight. You'll be a new lassie by this time tomorrow.'

I believed her. Already I felt stronger and unusually hungry. It was something that Gran seemed to realise would be an after effect of her treatment.

'Kitchen then lounge room, Tammy. Brew and scones suit you?'

I agreed, helping with the crockery and tea while Gran buttered some scones she'd made before the chaos of the day had unfolded.

After taking one mouth-watering bite, I inquired about them.

'Pumpkin,' she replied.

'What's it good for? Kidneys, memory, joints?'

'Nothing, my Tammy. It simply tastes nice. Saw it on an Australian cooking show. They make soup with it, too.'

I decided to revise my opinion of that country. They clearly did have something to offer apart from *Neighbours* and Paul Hogan. I'd once heard there was more culture in a pot of yogurt than the entire continent of Australia. Whatever the truth was, I decided that pumpkin scones were now right up there with Custard Creams.

Finally, we had time to talk properly. I chose to start with what was, to me, the more crucial question. We were seated side by side at each end of the brocade settee.

'Gran. What happened eleven years ago?'

Everything seemed to stem from that time; my illness, the row between my grandparents and Mum, the reason that I'd been cut out of Gran's life until now.

My grandmother fidgeted with her hands as she appeared to cast her mind back. I could imagine it was difficult for her.

'You were allus a precocious lass, speaking your mind. It was one of the qualities Horace and I admired in you. We could have taught you so much about the Valley to prepare you.'

Prepare me? For what? To be a guardian, like Gramps?

'We loved you, Tammy. We could see you had the potential to follow on in our footsteps. Sadly, your mother, bless her soul, didn't want that. Whether she was jealous or had her mind sozzled by too much drink . . . well, we'll never know. When you disappeared from the farm, she blamed us.'

There must have been some change in my expression that prompted her to ask.

'Tammy. You don't recall those days, do you?'

'Bits. Not much. That detective, Kim. I remember her, hugging me.'

Gran pondered on that, removing her glasses momentarily. She took a deep breath.

'Reight. That explains summat what's allus puzzled me. You were playing by the beck. Your gramps was chopping some trees down in Sherwood nearby. One minute you was there, next you was gone. We reckoned you wandered

77

off but, given events since, I believed you was snatched . . . taken. Though Lord knows why.'

'How long was I missing?' I wondered.

'Two days. We had the police and volunteers from as far off as Halifax, searching.

'Strangely when you reappeared, it was in Hebden. You were dazed yet in good health even if you were hungry. One of the police recognised you from your picture, down by the canal.'

'Kim?' Vague memories were stirring.

Gran nodded. 'Course, she was young — just starting out. We were so relieved — even though you had no recollection of what had happened. Almost like you'd been drugged. And no, nothing nasty had been done to you, if that's what you're thinking.'

I wasn't. Until then. For a moment, I had a hazy vision of a dark place near glowing water.

There was no chance I could have walked from Gran's house to Hebden

Bridge by myself. I'd damaged my knee the week before and had struggled to hobble a few yards.

'When I saw you had the Fairy Touch on your arm, I gave your Mum some on my salve. It should have cleared it up reight away.'

I recollected the blame and the fight between Mum and her parents. She'd gone ballistic. Mum had always been volatile. I now remembered she'd tossed a jar out of the car soon after taking me away from the area.

'I think Mum threw it away. Are you saying that if she'd used it on my arm, I wouldn't have had these past eleven years of pain and illness?'

This time Gran didn't respond. I wanted to hit someone . . . anyone. But Mum was dead now. Yet another thing to blame her for.

I swore loudly. Gran sat there waiting to hold me when I'd released all my pent-up anger. I sobbed my heart out as she hugged me.

'There, there, little Tammy.' She said

it quietly over and over. Inside I felt so angry. How could my own mother do that to me? She had to have known about Gran's skills with medicines and yet she'd thrown away my only hope of normal teenage years — and for what? Revenge? Spite? Blind ignorance?

At last, I was ready to move on. I took off my specs and dried my eyes again

'Sorry, Gran. I don't understand what came over me. I never get that emotional.'

Gran turned away from me and began whistling nonchalantly.

'Is there anything you haven't told me about your magic potions?' I asked. The whistling continued. 'Side effects, perhaps?'

'Er . . . Maybe I should have warned you, Tammy. Some of my patients have shown a smidgen of reaction to being cured of the Touch. With you, it might be a bit more.'

'Go on,' I urged, feeling like a cow wandering up to a barbecue then asking

'What's for dinner?'

'Mood changes. The Touch makes folk feel narky . . . depressed. It takes a while for the body to adjust. Tha might find thissen being affectionate or happy for no reason. Also, you might get words mixed up in your brain. Nowt serious, mind you.'

Gran was still showing a guilty face.

'And that's it? Nothing more?' I pressed her.

It was a whisper said quickly. I heard 'hair'.

'Sorry, Gran. What did you say about my hair?' She turned to face me, her eyes cast downward.

'You have to realise it hardly ever happens and when it does, it grows out in a year or two. Dyeing it don't work at all.' There was a lengthy pause. I crossed my arms and waited. 'It might turn . . . green.'

'Green?' I had sudden visions of being mistaken for a plant or *The Incredible Hulk*.

'Well, not bright green. More of a

chartreuse . . . turquoisey green. You'll hardly notice. Plus, I hear green is very trendy right now, Tammy.'

'For skirts and blouses, maybe. Not too sure about hair, Gran. Nevertheless, it'll be a small price to pay for you making me healthy again,' I said, trying to put her mind at ease. As for the hair, I'd cross that bridge when I came to it.

The bridge. I'd almost forgotten the jacket I'd found earlier. Darren was still missing and here was I, worried about a bad hair day.

I patted Gran's hand. She smiled at me. Although I'd been distracted by the past hour of hopefully ridding myself of the spots, it was time to ask about us again. It was at that moment I realised I'd not put my glasses back on, but now I could see the whole room clearly.

Gran must have realised it too. 'Seems like we got the Fairy Touch on the run, sweetheart.'

We chatted about that for a while until I chose to return to the reason we'd been separated all this time.

'Gran. I did write to you both. Did you never receive any of my cards and letters? One every birthday, to you both. I only discovered Gramps had died when Amanda rang me a few days ago. It was a horrible shock, to say the least.'

Gran put some more of the smelly cream on her hands before rubbing it in.

'I wrote too, sweetie. I assumed your mum tore them up or that you'd moved. Your father could never hold down a job. Like you with your grandpa, it was upsetting to hear about your mum. Not unexpected, though. She always had problems with alcohol, ever since she was in school. At least you're back in my life.'

I stood to walk to the front window with its views over the township of Hebden, the river Calder and the snake-like Rochdale Canal. It felt funny to be without my glasses. Almost like being naked.

'Where did the letters go? Someone

must have intercepted them. Someone who didn't want me back in your lives. If it hadn't been for Amanda's phone call . . . Where did you post them?'

'Hebden, of course,' my grandmother replied.

I checked my watch. Too late to go today. I'd leave it until tomorrow. Besides, I had my work to finish tonight and post off.

When Gran said she was feeling tired, I decided to ring Amanda to collect me. Gran was going to have some soup, then head off to bed.

Amanda told me twenty minutes. When I hung up, Gran asked if I could fetch some milk from the corner shop. I agreed happily, thinking to get some for us too, as the police visitors had depleted our supply.

★　★　★

I left Gran preparing her snack and headed off down the hill. It was still light with a double rainbow there to brighten up my frenetic day.

So much had happened — and now I'd changed also. No glasses and instead of the old me who'd walk down the street, barely lifting my eyes from the footpath, I was now confident and smiling. I was so preoccupied with the day's events, I didn't take any notice of the two people following me.

The street levelled out as we moved from the newer properties to the older terraced homes. There was no one else around as I approached the corner shop Gran had described.

Wonder if I should treat myself to some chocolate, I thought as I passed an alleyway, or ginnel as they called them up north. Just then I felt two hands grab my shoulders and shove me into the darkened space between two houses. A third hand pushed my head up against bricks, scraping my cheek against the cold roughness. Another closed over the only eye that could see anything.

'Don't look, Tamara Jordan,' a

huskily voiced woman shouted down my ear. She stank; a musty odour suffused with garlic. I sensed the other person was younger, male and very tough.

'You won't be hurt if you get out of Arcana Valley and Hebden and never contact your family again. Otherwise . . .'

I tried to struggle but their grips and pressure were far too strong.

'You can't threaten me.' My heart was racing and my throat was dry but I had to act strong.

'Ain't no threat, you nosey cow. Just a promise. Leave us and our treasure be. Get out . . . now.'

Then my I felt myself pushed, sending me sprawling onto the mossy, litter-strewn ground.

5

Gran applied some soothing salve to the abrasions on my face and legs. They felt better instantly.

'Shame you didn't see their faces, Tammy. No clues apart from there being a white older woman and a strong man?' Amanda demanded.

I thought as hard as I could. It was humiliating to be so helpless and intimidated, especially in broad daylight on a quiet street in an even quieter town. I should have done something. Yelled out, perhaps?

I had one further suggestion.

'She spoke with a local accent.'

'Oh wow. That narrows down the list of suspects, doesn't it? Shall we put out an All Points Bulletin? Tell Interpol to be on the lookout for . . . let's see . . . 'an older woman with a hoarse voice and a Yorkshire accent.''

She was covering her frustration with sarcasm.

Not that I could blame my aunt. She'd found me stumbling back up the hill, quite dazed. There'd been no sign of my assailants.

'That does it. I'm contacting Kim. We'll have an officer stationed outside here and back at the farm. I'm hardly capable of protecting you, Tammy — or Mum.' She tapped her stomach.

I sat down on the settee.

'My brain hurts. Too many strange things happening today.' I took a sip of fruit juice although a pint of cider would have been much more welcome.

While Amanda made her phone calls in the kitchen, I rested my head on my hands, seething with anger yet trying to put the jumbled pieces together. When Amanda returned it was time to discuss my thoughts.

'Whoever threatened me, knew my name, what I looked like and that I was at Gran's. They also mentioned treasure. They'd been waiting for me — but why not simply confront me and Gran together? Were they afraid Gran would recognise them? And why not simply ask me to leave?'

Amanda bent over to examine my injuries, noting that fortunately they weren't serious.

'One thing's for sure, Tammy. It seems to me that these threats are related to those missing letters between us,' said Gran.

'Missing letters?' asked Amanda.

We filled her in on our conclusions and my decision to investigate during my visit to the Post Office tomorrow. Although we could have mentioned those anonymous stuck-on messages to Gran, they weren't discussed. There was already too much going on with her life. Nevertheless, the Post Office visit might also be an opportune time to check on those Lady of the Lake stamps.

'I'm sorry but I have to go home to Uppermill tomorrow, Tammy,' my aunt apologised. 'Just for the day. I'll be back tomorrow evening.'

That meant I'd have to pursue my quest alone. Was I up to it? The answer was an emphatic 'yes'. Threats were one thing — but I'd just found my family again so there was no way I was walking away from them.

'Hey,' said Amanda. 'Where are your glasses, Tammy?'

Gran and I laughed. Regardless of the drama of the day, it felt good. Gran then explained how the treatment to cleanse me of the Fairy Touch had helped me already.

By the time we'd finished, a young policewoman had arrived. She'd keep Gran safe. As for us, it was time to go back to the farm, grab some food, finish my consultancy work then get some sleep.

Tomorrow would be time for Tammy 'Sherlock' Jordan to begin unravelling the mysteries of Arcana Valley.

★ ★ ★

Saturday was bright and sunny. I felt the same way. I'd left my glasses on the bedside table and was beginning to be quite used to not wearing them. Staring at the reflection in the bathroom mirror wasn't a drama either. There was colour in my cheeks, my hair was glossier with more bounce and I was ready to face the world. The abrasions from the previous evening were there but healing well.

I felt a little guilty when I thought about the huge meal I'd consumed last night, especially the three helpings of cheesecake. Gran had suggested that my appetite would increase until I reached normal weight, at which point I'd be reducing my meds.

I spent some time examining my hair. No split ends — and best of all, no tinges of green.

Amanda was already in the kitchen when I joined her. I methodically laid out my herbal supplements plus vitamins as 'prescribed' by my grandmother. I'd been surprised to discover she'd trained as a doctor during the war but was sidelined when the status quo of 'important jobs for men only' had resumed after 1945.

As we sat down to a hearty full English, Amanda commented on the array of vials set out in front of me.

'Folic acid? You're not pregnant too, Tammy?'

Folic acid was a B vitamin I was now using to counteract the anaemia caused by the Touch as it apparently helped with forming red blood cells.

'Ha! No chance,' I replied. 'I've had my share of men, thanks.'

'Not even that young policeman, Rick? I saw the way he kept glancing at you when he thought no one was noticing. If I weren't happily married, I could definitely add him to my wish list.'

'Well I don't. Fancy him, I mean. Could you imagine if I married him? Tammy Turpin? That sounds like a name for a Teletubby or a character from *Sesame Street*. As if . . . '

Amanda was staring at me, open-mouthed, her forkful of food poised in mid-air.

'I didn't suggest you getting married, Tammy. I'm surprised you've considered it. Gran told me you might be more open with your thoughts because of your treatment. Next thing you'll be telling me you had dreams about him.'

I tried not to react but my aunt was a trained watcher of people. I never stood a chance.

'Oh no. Don't say a thing. Too much information.' Then she burst out laughing. Soon, I was too.

When we stopped, Amanda had an observation.

'Tammy. This new uninhibited you is so much more fun than the old you. Wouldn't you agree?'

'Yeah. I simply have to remember not to open my mouth before thinking — especially if I see that Rick again. All we've really talked about was this missing guy. Not the most romantic of subjects. Any news on the investigation?'

'I checked with the officers who kept watch overnight. No sign of any intruders. As for forensics results, I don't expect we'll hear before Monday. Things tend to close down on the weekends and it's not as though it's time-crucial.' By that, she meant that no one had been killed yesterday.

After breakfast I made certain that my work was all packaged to post. I was well paid for my work, so I didn't feel guilty for cutting back on my workload for a while. Nevertheless, I decided not to go down to Tammy's bridge to check out progress myself. I wasn't a copper, as last night's feeble efforts to protect myself had shown.

As we drove to Hebden, I asked Amanda if she could give me some self-defence tips. She agreed, though she did point out she was hardly in a position to give hands-on demonstrations. She only had two weeks to go till the big day.

'You could ask Rick,' she suggested, grinning.

I wondered about that. The way my mind was behaving, I was like some giddy schoolgirl experiencing her first crush. My thoughts and feelings were all over the place.

I couldn't blame having too much alcohol this time. I hadn't touched a drop since Thursday.

Amanda hadn't been drinking as she was pregnant. I'd wondered if she disapproved of my attitude, especially considering that my mother, her only sister, had literally drunk herself to death. Perhaps it was time to take control of my own life, now that I'd been given a second chance.

The road to Hebden ran alongside Misty River for a mile or two. With the recent rain, the scenery was fresh and alive, dappled sunshine through the branches overhead giving the journey a peaceful ambience.

If I wasn't wearing my transition lenses any more, I'd need to buy some sunglasses pretty quickly. Perhaps I'd check out the town shops.

'Are you doing a shop today?' I asked my aunt as she adjusted the air-con in her car.

'Yes. Any particular requests? Something beginning with Custard perhaps?'

'Ha! No thanks.' I took three twenties from my handbag and popped them into her wallet.

We did a quick visit to Gran's to check on her. There was a policewoman sitting with her, someone I'd not seen before.

I planned to stay in town until Amanda came back. There should be enough to keep me busy. We each had our mobiles, in any case.

My aunt dropped me near the Post Office. It wasn't far from the river and historic canal. On entering, I was pleased to see that the two service windows were actually open. There was no one else there.

First things first; I arranged my work package to be sent special delivery and paid the required amount. Next, I asked to see the manager or manageress.

'That's me. Mr Butterball,' the older, grey-haired man declared. 'What seems to be the problem?'

'Missing mail. Over the period of the last eleven years. And it must have happened here.'

'That's a serious accusation, Miss. Do you have any proof?' he said officiously, drawing himself up to his full height of five foot six. His puffy cheeks became a Santa Claus red.

'If you mean, can I show you the letters that mysteriously disappeared? No. They're missing. In excess of thirty. I can give you some dates and you can answer my questions or not. It's up to you. Or maybe I could involve the police?'

That rattled him a little. He removed his wire rimmed glasses, gave them a meticulous polish then donned them again.

'I only started here a few months

ago, Miss. The previous postmistress has left. I can assure you that tampering with the mail is a serious offence. If you'd care to put all this in writing I can pass your letter on to our Theft Investigation Department.'

'Give you a letter. Oh yes. That worked so well with all the mail I sent to the Hathaways' box here over the years, none of which was delivered. If you can't help me, then perhaps I should speak with your predecessor. Could I have her name, please?'

'The Hathaways? You sent mail to them?' He glanced over to his male colleague who was also serving, perhaps seeking moral support. The younger guy seemed oblivious to our heated discussion. I guessed that he and Mr Butterball weren't on the best of terms. By this time, there was a queue of three customers and my voice had been raised too much.

At last, Mr Butterball regained his composure, putting both thumbs in his royal blue waistcoat pockets.

'I'm sorry, Miss. Personnel records are confidential. Now. If there's nothing more? We are very busy.'

He wouldn't look me in the eye. Damn. He knew something but had closed me down.

The only response I could think of was the one Arnie had used in *The Terminator*. I'd watched it on telly recently.

'I'll be back,' I stated with as much deep-throated conviction as I could manage.

* * *

I was cheesed off. Some detective I was! And the worst thing was, I was certain those letters being intercepted had something to do with this mysterious missing treasure trove and last night's not-so-veiled warning.

There weren't many people around as I made my way down to the canal path. Gramps used to bring me down here while Gran had her weekly shampoo and set. He said that watching the slow-moving boats there reminded him not to rush things.

Sometimes we'd just sit and watch the locks being opened and closed, as they were hundreds of years ago when the canal carried goods throughout the counties.

Finally, I reached one of the bridges that spanned the Rochdale Canal. I leaned over the stone wall, staring down at the tranquil waters. The ducks swimming there moved aside as a long canal boat appeared from under the arch, making its way leisurely away from me. A spaniel ran around the rear deck barking at the birds.

'It's an engineering miracle,' a man said from my side, startling from my daydream.

'Rick? DS Turpin? What are you doing here?'

The police officer was dressed casually, a white T-shirt and blue shorts complemented by trainers and short socks.

'Day off. I live in Hebden. Been jogging on the tow path.' He indicated the walkway alongside the canal where draught horses used to pull the boats laden with coal or provisions in bygone times. He must have come up behind me.

Although he'd claimed to have been running, there was no perspiration on his forehead. He wasn't overly muscular, though his lean body suited the tight T-shirt perfectly.

'Heard about your confrontation last night. How's the face now?'

I showed him and he took hold of my chin to move my head a little. His touch was gentle, his face close to mine. Was he thinking the same thing that I was?

At that moment I realised he was simply concerned. After all, I wasn't beautiful in any sense of the word. The indent of my glasses was still there on the bridge of my nose and . . .

'Yep. Nasty. But it's healing well. No dirt or gravel in it. You were lucky.'

We were facing one another now. He

hadn't moved away. Was this what they called the look of love? His chocolatey hair was neatly combed and trimmed, a widow's peak barely visible behind the part that fell down over his forehead.

'Hmmm. No glasses. Suits you.'

Well, he was a detective; a much better one than me. An idea pushed away my giddy love thoughts. I averted my eyes. It was time for work.

'Do you fancy a drink, Rick? There's something I'd like to discuss with you. I think it's relating to your crime.'

He checked his watch. 'I suppose. I've no plans for today.'

Then why did you check your watch? I wondered.

'My calves are aching from the workout so no more jogging today for me,' he went on. He lifted one foot to rest it on his knee. Then he massaged it with one hand, resting the other on my shoulder.

I winced.

'Apologies,' he said, straightening up. 'It's where that guy held you last night.'

'How did you know that? You weren't there.'

Or was he?

'I read the report, Tammy.' Rick gave a little laugh and I felt the tension disappear. Really — as if he could be involved!

He pointed to the blemish on my arm.

'That's fading. Can hardly see it now. Seems your gran has this Fairy Touch well in hand. She has quite a rep herabouts as a miracle worker. I'm pleased for you.'

So was I. It was the first time in years that I'd worn a short-sleeved shirt outside.

'Come on then, Tammy. There's a cafe down by the locks. Nowt special, but mind you, they do have great cakes.'

My face lit up. Cakes.

As we descended from the bridge to the towpath, Rick began to describe the town and canal's lengthy history. We crossed over a more substantial bridge which, in its time, must have been a phenomenon. The canal bridge flowed well above the river Calder that ran through the rocks below. I imagine how the sight of a barge almost flying through the air must have appeared to fishermen below.

The cafe's outdoor area overlooked the locks. A boat had just entered the lock from the lower level. As we ate and drank, we watched a woman winding a wheel to open the massive wooden gates leading to the higher canal level. The trickle of water became a torrent as the gates swung wider, filling the lock to raise the boat up.

She was strong. Despite having been focussed on her task, she now took a long pause to gaze all around. Having noticed us, she faced away, busying herself to the task in hand.

'Rick. Do you recognise that lady?' I nodded in her direction.

'Not sure. Maybe seen her around town. Redheads are fairly common around here.'

The person kept her face averted. Perhaps she was self-conscious. I could relate to that, having been somewhat of a recluse myself.

'What's so urgent you wanted to discuss with me, Tammy?'

I related the detailed story of the mail that had been intercepted between Gran and me, linking it to last night's threats. I clearly wasn't welcome here and hadn't been for some time. By the time I was finished, I had his attention.

He sat back on the metal chair, pensively.

'Sounds ominous. Any idea why? It's not as though you're special or important, is it?'

'Charming,' I replied with a feigned huff. 'Actually, I believe it's related to my disappearance back in the Eighties.'

'Oh yes. Little girl lost. DI Byrne mentioned that.'

By this time, the boat was level with the higher level of the canal. The reticent owner was back inside, navigating it from the lock. The boat was a dirty grey and green, apparently having been undercover during the recent storms. The name on the stern read *Mademoiselle A'Bor*.

'Perhaps we should return to the Post Office, Tammy? Sounds like they're hiding something.'

I was elated. My cunning plan to involve him in my investigation had succeeded.

Rick paid so we headed off. Mlle A'Bor was making a leisurely departure.

* * *

Mr Butterball was not impressed to see me again. When Rick introduced himself, showing his warrant card, he grudgingly became more compliant. He ushered us into a cramped office, piled high with overflowing file boxes and folders. He closed the door firmly before he plopped his rotund body into a swivel chair behind a heavy oak desk. We sat on the less comfortable folding chairs opposite.

'Our previous manageress, Mrs Griffiths, was dismissed for theft. Another employee discovered her secreting mail in her coat pocket, though Mrs Griffiths didn't suspect she'd been rumbled. The employee had suspected her for some time, though now she had proof. She rang Halifax who dispatched an investigator.

'Once the letter was found, Mrs Griffiths denied it. However a thorough search revealed a folder marked *Private* containing other letters to and from the Hathaways. Obviously, Mrs Griffiths was dismissed.'

'And that's it?' I was becoming upset.

'Of course not. There's a court case being prepared, although it was supposed to be low profile. You understand.' All the time he'd been addressing Rick; the usual assumption that a male was in charge of our team.

'No.' I was upset. 'I don't understand. Why weren't my grandmother or I informed? Where are the letters now? I can accept that this Griffiths thief was stupid enough to keep evidence of her crime — but for no one to tell us, the victims? That's inconceivable.'

At last I had his attention. He mopped his brow.

'We would have, Miss, but the mail was evidence and — '

Rick produced a small notebook from his T-shirt pocket. Not the sort of thing one would carry while jogging, I thought. He sat forward.

'Her full name and address, Mr Butterball. Now.'

Mr Butterball shifted on his chair, uneasily.

'Lois Griffiths. The Old Manor House, at the end of Misty River Road. She's moved, though. No forwarding address. I'd know,' he pointed out smugly. 'She lived in Arcana Valley. When her mail wasn't collected from her postbox here, one of our agents called. Deserted. Apart from more stolen mail and some other strange stuff.'

'Great.' I shook my head in disbelief.

Rick placed a calming hand on mine. It helped.

Rick was thinking more clearly.

'What about the employer whistle-blower? May we speak to her?'

'Dotty Smethurst. She's not in today,' Mr Butterball admitted. 'She will, however, be down at the old clog factory in Mytholmroyd. She has a little shop in the complex on the second floor.'

I looked at Rick. 'Do you know it?'

He nodded. 'We can go down there right now.'

'Then let's move.' I stood, eager to pursue the quest. But Rick wasn't quite finished.

'Mr Butterball. I want you to go to the local police station once you close up. You'll need to give a statement; everything you've told us. They'll be expecting you.'

'I can't do that. I'll require permission from head office and . . .'

Rick assumed a more dogmatic approach.

'Would you prefer me to request an area car and uniformed officers to come now?' He lifted out his mobile from the case attached to his belt.

'No . . . no. I'll be there. Voluntarily.' Rick smiled.

★ ★ ★

Once outside, Rick phoned the station. Kim was there and he gave her a thorough and succinct update. 'Miss Jordan and I will go to interview this Dotty person,' he said.

This didn't sound like normal police procedure. When he hung up, I asked him about it.

'Am I like a special constable now? Do I need to take an oath to uphold the law? Like doctors — they take a hypocritical oath, don't they?'

Rick stared at me before bursting into laughter.

'Hippocratic Oath. I thought you were smart?'

I wanted to protest that I was. It was

110

Gran's anti-Fairy Touch stuff. It was screwing up my emotions and memory big time.

Instead I stayed mum. He'd think it was a flimsy excuse.

I tried to think logically, like I used to. What Rick had said and done was well outside anything I'd expected. Some missing letters and a threat. Compared to investigating the kidnap, it made no sense at all. Moreover, if he thought I'd accept he was on a day's leave and had bumped into me by chance, he had another think coming.

'Rick. I'm not stupid. I'm having a few personal issues right now. You're keeping an eye on me and doing a pretty poor job of disguising the fact. Is there any development I should be aware of? After all, I'm the one in the middle of this mess.'

Rick sighed. 'Saw right through my little ruse, did you? OK. Last night we had news from the forensics team investigating Darren Bruce's belongings. They managed to reconstruct the water-damaged message on the till receipt. It said, *Help. Trapped glowing dark. Lo.* It appears it was rushed. He might have been interrupted. The last word was *LO*, not LOW.'

'*LO*? Initials . . . or Lois Griffiths?' I suggested.

Rick shrugged. 'Who knows? But it is worth investigating. She used to live upstream from where you found Darren Bruce's anorak. His car was dumped up that way. And she seems linked with you and your family with this stolen letter situation.'

I sensed there was something else the cute young detective wasn't disclosing. None of what he'd told me would have led to this degree of investigation.

'There is another reason, isn't there, Rick?'

'You're astute, Tammy. OK. As this whole complicated mess does seem to involve you and your family, I'll tell you. The powder stuff on Darren's possessions is some sort of glow-in-the-dark bacteria. There's only one other record of it on the forensics database.'

'Let me guess. Eleven years ago, on a young girl who'd been missing for two days . . . Me.'

6

There was a close connection between the missing letters and my disappearance all those years before. Also, last night's threats to leave the area and my family with that mention of the treasure; the same treasure, presumably, which Darren Bruce had been searching for.

They were all pieces of some intricate jigsaw. The trouble was there was no picture on the front of this jigsaw box to help me visualise how to fit the pieces together.

Rick took my hand.

'Are you OK, Tammy? You were pretty full-on in there. Are you always this intense?'

I decided it was best to tell a little white lie.

'It was an act, Rick. I've seen it on *The Bill*. Good cop. Bad cop. I'm usually as quiet as a church frog.'

That didn't sound right either. Were frogs quiet? Rick gave me a wary look and let go of my hand. Damn. He headed off and I followed.

'Shall we get down to the clog factory to interrogate this Dotty woman? I've never been in a police car . . . well, apart from that time your boss found me when I was twelve.'

'No police car, Tammy. We'll take mine. That's it over there.'

We'd rounded a corner. The only car in sight was an old VW Bug.

'No blues and twos?' I asked as he unlocked my door, which practically fell off as he opened it.

'Blues and . . . oh, you mean flashing lights and sirens? 'Fraid not. The exhaust is a bit noisy so people will probably notice us, don't worry.'

'Not your style then, Tammy?' Rick observed as I scrunched down to avoid the stares once we'd started.

'No. I'm more a convertible girl myself. Sports cars and all that.'

I was trying to sound sophisticated. Perhaps then he wouldn't be tempted to treat me like a dizzy blonde.

'I can put the roof down on this. Takes about ten minutes. We can stop to do that if you want.'

'No. It's OK.' The last thing I wanted was to be more conspicuous. 'Is it far?'

'A few miles. Next town along the canal, going towards Halifax. This mill used to be a clog factory.'

'I gathered that,' I said dryly. 'The name sort of gave it away.'

He seemed to not notice my sarcasm. 'Anyway, it still makes them for tourists and such. They used to wear them in the weaving mills throughout the area. Now there are lots of crafty and gift shops there. They even have the whole top floor decked out with Christmas displays the whole year round. Quite a local tourist attraction. Even a city girl like you might enjoy it.'

We drove in silence for the rest of the journey. I tried not to look at his bare legs in shorts as he changed gear but there wasn't much else to see. The windows on my side were dirty — so at least my identity was safe from all who turned to stare at this noisy relic from the Seventies.

★ ★ ★

The mill was literally at the side of the canal. I guess they used to unload raw materials and then send canal boats off laden with nineteenth — century wooden clogs in the latest fashion colours of muddy brown and coal-dust black.

As we walked into the massive brick mill, I asked Rick, 'How will we know which is her stall? We don't have any idea what she looks like.'

'The desk sergeant said her name is on the store front. Says she's quite a character.'

It didn't take us long to find her. *Dotty About Stamps* was tucked away between a Victorian tea room and a specialist model car shop. It was packed with stamps from around the world.

'Are you Dotty?' I asked the middle-aged woman with the most engaging smile.

'Mad as a March hare!' She laughed. 'Dotty by name. Dotty by nature.' Her dark eyes sparkled in the store spotlights. She had straight black hair and huge bifocals sitting half way down her nose.

'I'm from the police,' Rick said, showing her his ID. 'And this beautiful young lady is the grand-daughter of Mildred Hathaway. We wanted to ask you about Lois Griffiths.'

Dotty's sunny smile vanished.

'That thieving so-and-so. You. You're Tammy Jordan. You're the one whose letters were stolen. How can I help you?'

'It appears that Mrs Griffiths is now a person of interest in a kidnap inquiry. We would be grateful for any clues as to her whereabouts or photos of her, if you have any.'

Rick was doing his policeman thing again.

'She was a bit of a dark horse, was Lois. Kept herself to herself, if you ken. I only started at Hebden a few months before she was given the heave-ho. She broke the public's trust by stealing people's mail. I love working for the Post Office. Been doing it for donkey's years at other towns. Never did take to Lois, though. She was allus busy in that office of hers doing Lord knows what. A photo, you say? I think I have one taken by some reporter when we celebrated our refurbishment, installing those security screens about six months ago. Let me check my scrapbook.'

She rummaged under the counter for a minute then pulled out an album packed with scenes and information about her life working for the postal service, from her young days as a mailwoman to her present position. There, on the second last page, was a coloured photo of two women standing in front of the Hebden office.

There was no mistaking it, though Lois had her hair braided in a very old-fashioned style.

'I recognise her, Rick. It's that woman on the canal boat this morning.'

'You're certain, Tammy? I never saw her face.'

'Yep. That's her. Lois Flaming Griffiths. No wonder she looked guilty. It was probably her last night — the one who attacked me.'

It took a moment to sink in.

'I don't suppose I can take this to the station to get it copied?' Rick said to Dotty.

'You may, Detective Sergeant. If it helps catch Lois. I will like it back though.' Dotty carefully removed the photo from her album.

I followed up with another question.

'Did you realise she had a canal boat?'

'Nope. News to me. All I knew about was that wreck of a house she had in Arcana Valley. Used to be owned by one of the big landowners around here. Lord someone or other.'

We said our goodbyes. Then I

recalled the six bizarre letters. I'd brought one along.

'You're a philanthropist, aren't you, Dotty?'

She stared at me, as did Rick. Then her features brightened. I'd used the wrong word again.

'I think you mean philatelist, Miss. Yes. I love my stamps. Why?'

I showed her the envelope that had the cut-up lettered message inside.

'This is the Lady of the Lake issued in 1985, isn't it?'

Dotty examined the stamp depicting a white-clad woman lifting Excalibur from the waters.

'Oh yes. Not that common. Set of four, if I remember. What about it?'

'I don't suppose you've noticed other letters using it being mailed at Hebden?'

If the perpetrator of the anonymous riddles had sent other letters using the same stamp, we had a chance of tracking them down.

Dotty peered down at the stamp through her bifocals, then up at us, then to her filing cabinet.

'I wonder.' She was very pensive. 'February? Yes, it was February. Some of my regulars bring me envelopes with stamps on them. The rarer ones I keep for my shop, the others I give to charity.' She went to the cabinet and shuffled through it.

'Ah yes. Here it is. Lady of the Lake; two twenty-two pence stamps, just like your letter. Placed in the same way. I don't have the address of the sender but perhaps the person to whom it was sent will remember.'

'Who's that then?' Rick inquired.

I tapped the envelope with an address on it. Rick read it sheepishly.

'Some detective you are.' I grinned.

★ ★ ★

Before we headed off to interview the letter's owner, I insisted on a proper lunch at the tea shop next door. I was famished and had decided that detectiving was very, very hard work.

122

In addition, it was time to discover what made DS Turpin tick. What were his hobbies? Did he enjoy listening to Oasis? And did he fancy twenty-three-year-old blondes named Tammy?

First port of call was the ladies to apply some of Gran's cream. Now, had she said once a day or three times? I couldn't wait for this memory fog side effect to run its course. To be on the safe side, I put some on. It wasn't as if it was some strong tablet. Finally, a lipstick top-up. Fuchsia pink. I kept one in my pocket for emergencies . . . and this certainly qualified.

Then Rick and I sat down for our meal. Discovering that he did like Oasis, I felt ecstatic. We were clearly meant to be together. Unfortunately, he admitted to liking The Beautiful South as well, though I could tolerate that . . . just.

He had a fresh, almost boyish face though his eyes were resolute and determined. All the time he was glancing around, observing our fellow diners and passers-by. Whether he was watching for possible threats to me or if it was normal for him, I could only guess. Even so, it was reassuring to have him with me, especially after last night's threats. They'd shaken me up.

I didn't take notice of any of the other people. There was only one person on my mind. Conscious that it was rude to stare, I examined his tanned arms and hands. His nails were neatly trimmed, his watch was a Pulsar . . .

'Tammy. Are you OK?'

'Yes. Just a bit woozy. Is my hair green?'

'No. It's normal blonde. Why?'

I took a long drink of water. Darn. What was wrong with me?

'I asked you about your life in Manchester. Must be pretty exciting. All those clubs and such.'

I was feeling a bit better now.

'I don't really bother mixing with people. It suits me to live there because I can keep to myself. I'm one person among thousands. Out in a place like this, I have to interact more. It's more difficult to hide. All of a sudden, I have Amanda and Gran in my life.'

'No one else, then? Boyfriend? Girlfriend? Pet goldfish?'

'There was Rooster,' I confessed. 'His proper name was Kyle. Wasn't really a boyfriend, though he liked me. I simply thought of him as a friend. We're finished now. He became a bit of a pest in the end. What about you, Rick? Married?'

He hesitated. 'I have a girlfriend. Rose . . . she's a school teacher. Primary. She's away this weekend.'

'That's nice.' I averted my eyes.

I took a deep breath. There was still work to do and people to question. I took the envelope Dotty had given us from my handbag.

'Ready?' I said, standing up.

'But I thought you wanted dessert, Tammy.'

'Lost my appetite.'

We paid and left. Rick knew the

address on the envelope, so we set off in his car. I wasn't bothered if anyone saw me now. All I wanted was to get on with my life.

★ ★ ★

The house we went to was on the way to Hardcastle Crags which, according to Rick was a beautiful riverside picnic spot. I thought enviously of him going there with his precious Rose.

It was a wasted journey. The owner of the envelope couldn't help us. He was a widower whose wife had passed away around the same time as the date stamp on the envelope.

'I had so many cards from friends and relatives, DS Turpin. I can't remember who sent that one. It was a difficult time for me.'

'I understand,' Rick said gently. 'However, if I might take your phone number, Mr Bertanelli? Just in case.'

He gave the old man his own card and we drove back to the Hebden police station where I was given a Visitor pass. By this time, I was feeling as rough as a hedgehog's back.

Rick sat me down in an empty interview room.

'You look a bit off-colour, Tammy. I'll get you another drink.'

Quite frankly I didn't care what I appeared to be any longer. Dreadful summed up the way my stomach was behaving. I was certain that green hair would have been a preferable side effect.

He returned with a glass of iced water — and Kim.

'Tammy. We need to talk,' she announced, pulling up a chair. 'But firstly, I need you to take this. Your gran prepared it.'

'Great,' I said, regarding the small vial of purple liquid. 'What is it this time? Liquefied dragon's tongues?'

Rick sat down opposite me, his face showing real compassion.

'It's to stabilise your emotions, Tammy. Without wanting to be rude, you've been all over the place today. Sometimes you're incisive and a well-adjusted adult, other times you're like a belligerent teenager.

'If I hadn't been forewarned about what was going on, I would have left you back at the Post Office. You've used too much of that ointment. There's been a battle between the Fairy Touch and the cure, with the real Tammy Jordan stuck in the middle.'

I hadn't felt right for the last hour or so but, in retrospect, today had been a rollercoaster of feelings. Maybe I had overdone the ointment.

'Sorry, Rick. Give me the dragon's tongue, then. Anything's better than feeling like this. And I really hope you and your Rose are very happy together . . .'

'Best leave her for a few minutes, DS Turpin. I'll come outside with you so you can explain what you've discovered — and about this girlfriend of yours. I trust you'll have satisfactory answers.'

'But I . . . I . . . ' Rick said in a panic.

128

'Nothing happened. It's all in her head.'

'Sure. And I'm the Easter Bunny. Outside, mister. Now.'

The door closed noisily as I sat, head in hands. The last day played over and over in my mind, reminding me how absolutely deranged I must have appeared. I only hoped I'd not hurt anyone by my behaviour. As for facing Rick again, I owed him a huge apology. No one likes unwanted attention. I'd discovered that myself with Rooster and his obsession with controlling me. Thank goodness he didn't know where I'd moved to.

I finally felt strong enough to face the music. I left the room. A young female officer was awaiting me. She guided me through more corridors to the Incident Room.

You can imagine how surprised I was to see my gran and Amanda standing there.

'Sleeping Beauty has arrived,' Rick announced on seeing me.

'I have to apologise to you all,' I said

as Gran wandered over to be with Kim and Rick. Amanda remained seated, understandably. 'I've been behaving like — '

'A mad dog?' Kim suggested.

'A giddy schoolgirl?' chirped up Rick.

'My gorgeous granddaughter struggling to be the woman she should be.' Gran grinned. 'I had no idea that all of that would happen. Then again, I've never had to eradicate such a deep-rooted infection of the Touch. Promise me one thing, sweetheart. You'll leave the application of the vitamins and poultices to us from now on. Clearly your brain went a bit fruit-loopy.'

'I promise, Gran. Trouble is I'm not sure how impartial I can be, judging by my behaviour. All day I was thinking that whatever I said or did was perfectly fine. You did warn me, but even so . . . many apologies, guys.'

Kim came over to hug me.

'Rest assured. We'll tell you if you're being a wally, Tammy. Now, if you're ready, it's time to put that mind of yours to work. You are a Guardian of the Valley after all — even though you might not realise it.'

I was stunned. 'What? Like Gramps?' I said.

Gran nodded. 'You have to understand that it's not a genetic thing — you don't have superpowers or owt. Your role, like most of us here, is to sort of look after things. Keep the status quo. Guard the Secrets.'

'Secrets. Like what?' I was intrigued.

'If we told you that, they wouldn't be secrets, would they, lass? You'll learn some of them in time. Some, even we don't know.'

I glanced at the three of them in turn.

'You're some sort of squad then, protecting things — like the police? That woman last night . . . Lois . . . told me to stay away from her treasure.'

'We've been around long before the police. Since the 1500s. And those riches she mentioned must be the Thesaurus Crucis, or Treasure of the

Cross,' said Rick.

I thought about that. 'I wondered why there was never any suggestion that Gran, Amanda or I were involved in this abduction. I assume that's why I'm here now. Care to fill me in?'

We all moved to sit around the table. Gran took charge, confirming she was the de-facto leader of this clandestine group.

'Before we begin there's something that needs to be said and it involves you, my dearest granddaughter, and Rick.'

While I suspected she'd do that, Rick immediately became defensive.

Gran continued, staring at both of us in turn.

'The tension between you two is overpowering and has to be resolved.'

Even I was aghast at that comment.

'Gran!'

My gran's eyes opened wide.

'No. Not like that, Tammy — even though I suspect that's what you want.'

I blushed and bit my lip before

muttering, 'Rick already has a girl-friend. A teacher called Rose.'

Everyone faced Rick, who must have felt so intimidated by four women awaiting his response.

'There is no girlfriend. I made her up to make you back off, Tammy. You were being weird.'

'I wasn't weird,' I protested.

'You asked me if you had green hair, Tammy. You were coming on like a lovestruck teenager. I had to say something.'

It was uncomfortable saying all of this in front of my aunt, Gran and Kim but it did need saying. If only they weren't grinning so much.

'OK. I admit it. I like you, Rick. Most guys ignore me but you didn't, even despite my skin problems. I've never had a real boyfriend. When I began to feel better last night, other things happened too — feelings I'd never had before. And they involved you. I'm sorry.'

Rick listened. He was good at doing that.

'I like you too, Tammy. Well, more than like. Yesterday we had, a connection but today, you were creepy. As I said, if your gran and my DI hadn't warned me . . . '

Gran explained. 'The Fairy Touch affects the body. The real Tammy's thoughts have been supressed for so long that she'd lost the self-confidence she'd had as a girl. As for her compassion, that won't change. And I believe today's behaviour has been a one-off. Her body is mending. She no longer needs glasses, her appetite and general health will stabilise and she will re-emerge as a beautiful woman, in body and mind. However, might I suggest that the mutual attraction you two clearly have for one another be reined in until we get this crime solved; finding Darren and reuniting him with his wife and bairns.'

I exchanged a covert glance with Rick and sighed. Gran was right; other things were more important right now.

'OK. What do we have? I want to

know the whole story about this treasure. It's the key to finding Darren. I'm positive.'

* * *

My mind was alert — more so than I could ever remember it bring It was as if a part of me had been dormant for the past eleven years since that kidnap.

If Gran hadn't begun her cure, I'd still be the sickly, insipid, mixed-up person I'd been for years. Now, I was sure I could be so much more.

Kim was about to point out items on the Action Board when Gran interrupted.

'I reckon our Sleeping Beauty has sussed it out. Yes, Tammy. You've been manipulated by persons unknown ever since you was taken away, eleven years ago. It's been a long-term scheme to keep you away from the Valley.'

'Me? Why?'

'Because whoever it is behind all this has been scared of what you would become. They knew your potential.'

'Then why not just kill me, back when I was twelve? Why send me home, infected?'

There was silence. It was Kim who told me.

'We don't understand that ourselves. Perhaps they needed you for something but not at your full strength. Or perhaps they are simply not killers.'

It was a lot to take in.

Time for me to discover the latest information.

'The woman on the canal boat — Lois Griffiths. Have you found her?'

Kim looked guilty. 'No. Can't understand it but she and her boat — Mademoiselle A'Bor? — have vanished. Nowhere to be found. We've checked right up to Halifax and back past Rochdale. Unless she has an outboard motor strapped to it, there's no way she could vanish that quickly.'

I thought. 'Disguised? Hiding in a tributary?'

'We thought of that. No trace.'

'What about Lois's house in the Valley?'

'Cleared out. Apart from rubbish and incidentals. We're processing them.'

'So. At this stage finding her is a dead end. She appears to have gone to ground. The next thing is Darren's possessions. Any news there?'

'Not really.' Kim indicated the board covered in photos and handwritten notes.

Gran added more information.

'The Fairy Touch is only found in the Valley — and in people born there. Like you, Tammy.'

I hadn't realised that.

Gran shifted on the uncomfortable chair. Kim went outside and returned with a cushion.

'For the benefit of the two young 'uns here, I'm going to start at the beginning. All of this began with the Reformation back in the 1500s. The Knights Hospitaller had a Preceptory in Newland near Wakefield and, rather than let their wealth be stolen by Henry

VIII, they hid it in Arcana Valley. The area was isolated and had been recently ravaged by the Bubonic Plague or Black Death.'

I made a note about the cut-out letter referencing Ring-a-ring-a-rosie, and the stone memorial Kim had found at Gran's farm in Sherwood Forest.

'The story goes that the Treasure of the Cross was secreted underground near a large body of water and was never recovered. Guardians were appointed to prevent the gold and such being stolen. I'm one of them and now, Tammy is too. The trouble is, over the centuries, the location has been lost. Not a bad thing if we want it to stay hidden, mind you.'

I couldn't help myself.

'So, I'm a Guardian with nothing to guard?'

Gran's stare of annoyance at being interrupted put me in my place again.

'There was a local family intent on discovering and taking the treasure for themselves, the most notorious member being Lord Nibberton in the early 1800s. He helped finance the Rochdale Canal construction between Rochdale and Halifax. By all accounts, he was an evil despot. Lois Griffiths was living in the remains of his Manor House in the Valley. I now believe she's searching for the Thesaurus Crucis and has abducted Darren Bruce to assist her in her nefarious quest.'

She sat back.

'Gran,' I ventured. 'We found some cryptic letters alluding to someone discovering the treasure. Cut-out letters stuck on pages, posted to you and Gramps. There were six of them.'

Gran's eyes lit up.

'Ah. The mysterious letters. I wondered where they went. No idea who sent them.'

I waved the envelope Dotty had given us.

'This one seems to have been sent by the same individual. He or she used the same Lady of the Lake stamps from 1985. The recipient, Mr Bertanelli, had no idea who'd sent it, either. His wife had just passed away and he told us there were a lot of condolence cards.'

Gran explained a bit more.

'We kept them 'cause Gramps liked the stamps. They seemed important but we could never suss them out. Could have used your brains back then, Tammy.'

Fingering the envelope, I realised it wasn't the shape of those that usually held cards . . .

'Rick,' I speculated with a tinge of excitement. 'Could you ring Mr Bertanelli for me? You have his number.'

Rick dialled and passed the phone to me.

'Hello, Mr Bertanelli. It's Tammy. I was with DS Turpin this afternoon. Remember? . . . I'm wondering if you could tell me the name of the funeral director you dealt with for your wife's funeral?' I thanked him before turning to my grandmother.

'Do you know a man named Cyril Andover?'

'Why, yes. Young Cyril. A long, long time ago. Must be getting on a bit now.'

I faced the rest of our small team and smiled.

'That's the connection. I'm guessing Cyril Andover found the treasure and wanted to tell someone about it. Someone he knew would keep the secret because he knew she was a Guardian. You, Gran. That's why he sent you those letters.'

7

I felt their doubt, but also strong belief in whatever skills I apparently had. It was strange to be thought of in that way. All of my teenage and adult life I'd been treated with pity or scorn. No wonder I'd become a recluse working at home by myself, hiding in a city full of total strangers.

'I believe those letters are important. They will tell us where the treasure is — and hopefully where Darren is, too. At the very least, if we find the treasure first, there will be no need for this Lois Griffiths to keep him. She'll have to let him go before disappearing from the area.'

There was always the possibility that she wouldn't let him go — but my instinct told me that just as I'd been released eleven years before, Darren would be also. Lois had kept my gran and me apart for all those years; it was logical that it was she who'd kidnapped me back then.

Lois Griffiths had ruined my life. There was no way I'd let her do any more evil things.

'May I use this blank whiteboard?'

Kim gestured. 'Be our guest, Miss Sherlock.'

'We haven't got the letters here to read what they say,' Rick pointed out.

'No problem. I know them all off by heart.'

I wrote out the cryptic phrases.

Ring a ring a rosie.

When 'tis silin', off bleggin', eyen the goosegogs, thissen.

Today's the day Teddy has his picnic.

Gold coins, silver coins, shiny jewels and treasure. Hidden by the church men, discovered at my leisure.

Who's afraid of the big, bad wolf? Vervain won't save her now.

Remember the promise, Mildred Hathaway.

The last message had been delivered first. Next to them I wrote *Lady of the Lake stamps*.

'And finally, we have Mr Bertanelli's envelope with the same stamps. The one he received when his wife died earlier this year.'

I stood, marker pen in hand, waiting.

Rick spun around on his swivel chair and began typing on the police computer at one end of the room. We waited expectantly. 'Cyril Andover, funeral director, passed away in April this year aged seventy. That letter to Mr Bertanelli was probably the funeral bill from Cyril who himself died soon after. The last message letter to Mrs Hathaway was dated March.'

Gran was clearly agitated.

'I'm sorry. I don't understand, Tammy. Are you saying that little Cyril sent us funny messages? It don't make sense. Why not just tell me and Gramps straight out?'

I wondered whether, given her distress, she really had to be here before realising that we needed her recollections to solve this conundrum.

'Gran. It says on one of the notes, *Remember the promise, Mildred Hathaway*. What promise?'

Gran seemed angry, more at herself than me. Her memory wasn't what it had once been and I could sense her frustration.

'Back then, in the Twenties and early Thirties there was a gang of us bairns. We went to school together and all lived in Arcana Valley. Cyril was one of them. Not your Gramps, though. We young 'uns would spend all our spare time playing, often at our farm.'

'And in Sherwood Forest?' Rick suggested.

'Yes. As I recollect, we did. Used to swim in the stream, too. Can't recall no promise, though. Cyril was the youngest boy. He loved playing there with all of us.'

I was trying to reason it through.

'Possibly he made you agree to something so childish and daft and you simply thought he was kidding. You agreed to always be friends or keep in touch or look out for one another. Maybe that's what he did.'

Gran considered my suggestion.

'Cyril . . . Well. He had a tough time at home. Used to tell riddles and jokes all the time to make up for it, trying to make hissen happy. I guess to someone trying to recall happier times, being here with me would be the place. He once told me a terrible secret about his family. Made me promise to tell no one — though I don't think it matters now that Cyril's passed. I was the only one he'd tell his secrets to.'

Kim sat back in her swivel chair, interlocking her fingers.

'It's so unbelievable, yet it all makes sense.' She stood up to shake my hand.

'Confiding secrets to you by riddles. You've done it, Tammy. You saw the answer intuitively.'

'Her Gramps did the same thing. He called it his Leap of Faith. Looks like Tammy has his gift.'

The more I thought about it, the more it made sense. I couldn't understand how my mind was now this sharp. I examined my arm. The marks were barely discernible now. Could I have always felt this well, confident and smart, had it not been the Fairy Touch? That flipping Lois Griffiths had a lot to answer for. She'd kept me apart from my family — and for all I knew, she might have been the one who infected me all those years ago.

★ ★ ★

We decided Gran should come home with us that evening. We had a much better chance of getting answers sifting through generations of accumulated Valley history if she were there. Plus, I wanted her safe with us.

After we put the shopping away, Gran decided a few hours' sleep were in order.

'I'm no spring chicken any longer, more's the pity. Saying that, in my heyday I could have given that Rick fellow summat to remember.'

Later, as we put the groceries away, I saw Amanda opening a box.

'What have you got there?'

She was shuffling through some floppy discs.

'A few files I brought from home. I brought my computer, too. Can you give me a hand to bring it in from the car and connect it up?'

'Computer? Here?'

'Gran's phone line is fine for a modem. We should be online in half an hour.'

'You're kidding. Are you telling me, I can check my emails from here?'

'If you want. Gran's taken her computer to her new home so I needed mine here.'

I was shocked. I never imagined my grandmother was so progressive. And now, if we could go online here, I could catch up on my own work. There was no reason to go home, apart from fetching some files — and more clothes.

Wearing the same three blouses over and over was becoming tedious.

As Amanda was with child, I had to do the heavy lifting plus crawl around on the floor connecting cables and leads. The monitor was heavy. I'd read about Apple bringing out a portable computer which might be more sensible for me than being tied down to one place.

After Amanda settled down to typing, I decided to take a walk down to the crime scene. It was a warm, sunny afternoon with a cool breeze coming from the north. I felt more alive than I had in ages and had borrowed some of Amanda's sunglasses. I doubted I'd ever use my prescription specs again — at least, not until I was much older.

The brook was flowing more gently now, down towards my bridge and the barrier of tape printed with the warning *Police Line. Do Not Cross.*

A movement caught the corner of my eye. I read once that our peripheral vision was highly sensitive to movement; a legacy of evolution protecting us from danger.

A uniformed officer appeared.

'You shouldn't be here . . . oh, it's you, Miss Jordan. I didn't realise.' His accent was from north of the borders.

'Are you the only one here now, Constable . . . ?'

'MacDonald, Miss. Steve. Yes. DI Byrne wanted me to keep an eye on the site . . . and on you ladies.'

'Steve MacDonald. Like in *Coronation Street*? Not that I watch it at all, Constable. Even if I do live in Manchester.'

He took off his peaked cap. He had a closely shaved head and looked quite similar to that guy from *Die Hard* and the telly show *Moonlighting*. His eyes were narrow and blue. He was also a good six foot three in height.

I decided he wasn't the sort for any criminal to mess with. Rick had a much kinder face, though I suspected that he'd be more than capable of defending himself too.

'Don't go past the tape, please, Miss. The forensic boffins haven't finished with the area.'

'I understand, officer.'

He nodded, then made his way towards the police vehicle I could just see through the trees.

That left me free to approach the tree-line. All around were signs of the recent tempest's damage — broken branches strewn everywhere.

It was difficult to believe I'd only found the coat yesterday. So much had happened. Whereas then I'd been timid and introverted, I now felt a quiet confidence suffusing me. It wasn't arrogance, more a strength in both my body and mind that changed me from one of life's victims to someone who could think clearly in a crisis.

My head was still crammed with all that information I'd read. When I'd been ill and off school, my mother's solution to the inconvenience of having me at home had always been to give me some encyclopaedia or reference book to read.

There had been one article I'd read years ago that seemed to sum up the change in me now that the Fairy Touch was disappearing from my system. Gran had told me that once it was weaker, my own immune system would step up to fight it too.

The article had been written by an ex-mugger, a thief who preyed on innocent people on the streets. He'd weighed up his potential victims based on their body language. Those that walked along, head down, avoiding eye contact were much less likely to put up a struggle than those who constantly watched their surroundings. I'd always been one of the former.

Well, no longer. It was time to take charge of my life. I had done OK with my job already, but some self-defence training was a priority.

Gazing into the copse, I wondered why a memorial to those poor Black Death victims was in there. Was it the site of an old Catholic church? Part of me could still sense something supernatural about this place but right now, I had more pressing matters to tend to.

It was time to return to the house.

Whether it was some sixth sense or the sound of something not quite right, I fell to the grass. An object whizzed over my body, hitting a tree in the fenced-off zone. Scrambling to run, crouched low behind some cover, I screamed out for help, over and over. An arrow landed feet away.

From ahead, there was the sound of boots crashing through undergrowth. I was trapped and defenceless. Another arrow hit the rock I was sheltering behind with a flash, sending chips of rock showering over me.

My heart was thumping hard as I cowered behind bushes and boulders, trying frantically to hide. I needed a weapon — but what?

Just then some twigs snapped from beside me. There was a hooded figure, pointing a notched arrow at my feet.

'Help me!' I screamed again, as loudly as I could, as my fingers searched the leaf litter.

'You were warned to leave, lady,' a gruff male voice told me. He began to move the point of the arrow further up my body, seemingly taking delight in my fear.

I grovelled, pretending to beg for mercy then, grabbing a large rock with both hands, I thumped it down on his scruffy trainers. He screamed but it didn't stop him pulling back the bowstring, calling me every filthy name under the sun.

Lifting the rock again, it was clear there wasn't time for another strike at my assailant.

'NOOOO!' I screamed as I lunged at him.

8

A gunshot rang out overhead. We both turned. In the distance I could see a dark blue uniformed officer crouching with a gun pointed towards us.

'Police. Drop your weapon.'

My assailant hesitated before letting his bow and arrow tumble to the ground. Then, despite his foot wound, he loped away into the dense under-growth. I breathed a sigh of relief.

It took the officer an age to run up to my side.

'Quick. He's getting away.'

The policeman scanned the bushes for any sign before kneeling down to help me to my feet.

'Let him. I need to get you to safety.'

'At least call it in. The madman tried to kill me. If it hadn't been for you . . . ' I stood up to hug him. 'Thank you.'

He retrieved the bow gingerly,

concerned not to smudge any finger-prints. My assailant had been wearing gloves but perhaps there might have been some from earlier. It was a compound bow made of fibreglass and aluminium.

The constable gave a succinct report on the radio, including a description of Robin Hood.

'I injured his foot,' I said, pointing to the bloodied rock on the dirt. He added *Might be limping* and *Hospital watch* to his report, requesting DI Byrne be notified immediately.

'Well done on fighting back, Miss Jordan. I bet he wasn't expecting that. I heard you, but tripped over as I was running here. Good thing I was armed. DI Byrne insisted on it.'

'You could have shot him.'

'No, Miss Jordan. Not from that distance. It was a bluff. Now let's get you back to the house. Are you injured at all? I can get an ambulance.'

'No. A bit shaken. Nothing two pints of cider won't fix.' He stared at me.

'Just kidding, officer.'

In actual fact, I had never felt less like drinking. I'd realised that my habits had become too much like my mother's. Like mother, like daughter? She hadn't been the best of role models.

In the distance, I could hear a car starting up. Robin Hood making his getaway. Hopefully he'd be caught, as there weren't many places to drive to out here.

By the time we'd made our way back, two other police cars had arrived and officers were searching the area.

Kim arrived soon after. She talked to Constable MacDonald before sending him back outside to aid the search for evidence. There were the three arrows, for starters. Finally, she turned to me, Amanda and a very concerned-looking Gran.

'Flaming hell, Tammy. Can't leave you alone for a minute. You must have really cheesed someone off, big time.'

'Lois Griffiths?' I asked Kim.

'Seems likely, but let's keep an open mind.'

I took a sip of the coffee that Amanda had prepared, almost spilling it as it was too hot.

'Reckon Lois is getting crossed off my Christmas card list, whatever. Any news on her canal boat?'

'Nope,' Kim replied. 'Vanished like those planes and boats in the Bermuda Triangle. I'm going to take another run out to her abandoned home tomorrow. I'd like you with me, if you feel up to it.'

'Yeah, why not? A visit to a creepy old house in Spooky Valley where a homicidal maniac once lived sounds like a perfect Sunday outing. Shall I pack a picnic?'

Kim gave a broad smile.

'I like your attitude, Tammy.'

'No more Miss Nice Girl. Whatever it takes to sort out this nightmare, Inspector, count me in.'

'Good. I'm stationing a policewoman to stay here overnight and I'll see you tomorrow at nine. Dress appropriately.'

'Will Rick . . . er, I mean Detective Sergeant Turpin be coming?'

Kim eyed me questioningly.

'No. He's on leave tomorrow.'

'Like he was today?' I asked, nonchalantly.

'No. He was pretending today, as well you've guessed. He didn't want to alarm you but we needed to watch you. Something big is happening in Arcana Valley right now and, for some reason, it centres around you.'

* * *

After putting another splodge of ointment on me that evening, Gran told me she'd stay here with us as she felt safer. Her old bed was still made up, as Amanda and I had been using the spare bedrooms.

I'd been using the room I'd slept in whenever I stayed here as a child. It still had the same wallpaper and calming ambience I recalled from those happy holidays.

'Amanda and I will try to find the paperwork that Annabelle wanted. I know it's around here someplace. Also, there are those letters with the cut-up writing. There's some message Cyril was teasing us with. We'll try to decipher what he was trying to say. I cannot believe he'd do that — though he always was a strange one.'

'Actually, Gran, I've decided to go back home on Monday.'

My grandmother was aghast.

'Home? You're not seeing this mess through with us, Tammy?'

'Oh, I am. I just need to check my work back in Manchester and bring it back with me. Plus, I've decided to go to the big library there in St Peter's Square. I want to do my own research on the area, especially the canals. I have a hunch that this puzzle is connected with them in some way.'

That image in my memory of the shining water in the dark was a mirror of the place where Darren must have been when he wrote that message and dropped his anorak into the water.

Amanda came back in from giving the officers outside a bite to eat.

'What's that about canals? Where I live in Uppermill, we can see the canal quite clearly.'

'Same with me,' I added. That wasn't a coincidence either, I decided. It was as though something drew us to the waterway like a magnet.

'But here, in the Valley, we're miles from the Rochdale Canal,' Gran added.

The young policewoman seated near the front door yelled out something.

'Sorry, Karen. Couldn't quite hear you,' Amanda called back.

We heard the radio squawk as she checked with her colleagues, then she walked into the lounge. The room was still piled high with boxes.

'Sorry for eavesdropping. I was just saying, there are the remains of canals nearby. Tributaries to the one through Hebden. They're dried up and mostly derelict, but they're there. Used to play in them when I was a kid.'

Her radio came to life again. She excused herself and returned a few moments later.

'Just to let you in on the latest. They've arrested your assailant, Miss Jordan. Seemed he went into Calderdale Royal Hospital in Halifax, claiming he'd stood on a nail. When the doctors pointed out that his wound was from the top of his foot and not underneath, he tried to make a limp for it. Didn't get far. He's been patched up and is in custody. DS Turpin is interviewing him now. He claims it was all a joke that went wrong.'

'Some joke,' I said, with an angry scowl.

'Thanks for the update, Constable,' Amanda told her. 'The threat isn't past, though, so stay alert. Pass it on.'

★ ★ ★

That evening was pleasantly uneventful. Having three generations of our family together was relaxing and cathartic for me. They were indeed the family I'd always craved, laughing at memories like the time I'd been convinced I'd seen a dragon in Misty River while we were all swimming there.

Amanda chuckled. 'What on earth were you thinking, Tammy? That we were in Loch Ness?'

At other times, it was sobering as I told Gran and Amanda about those last few hours in hospital following the car crash that killed my parents. Mum had been driving. Her blood test had revealed the unsurprising cause. Nevertheless, seeing her there, wired up to all those machines in the time before she'd passed away . . .

I should have tried to find a phone number to ring Gran and Gramps in the hope of a final reconciliation, but I didn't. If my grandparents had never written and had never answered my correspondence, I'd been certain that they had no interest in us any longer.

In retrospect, I'd been wrong to believe that. It had been Lois's heinous actions in stealing the mail that had convinced me that I'd been forgotten. I hated her.

Gran reminisced about Mum as a girl, so full of enthusiasm and joy. Gramps had wanted her to follow in his footsteps as a Guardian and she would have done, had she not met my father and lost her way. After I was born, Gramps saw another chance with me and it had gone well until the time I'd gone missing. That's when Mum had taken me away.

I had to know. Mum had never talked about that day.

'Gran. What happened between you?'

She was reluctant to answer. I was forcing her to relive painful memories. Amanda had been away at the time, training with the police.

'When that Kim policewoman brought you home, your mother accused us of neglect and a great deal more. She was reight mardy, screaming that she'd been told what the secret of Arcana Valley really was and that she wanted nowt to do with it or my witchcraft. I'd seen that you had the Touch on your arm, so I gave her some herbal cream to rid you of it but that set her off even more. That's the last I saw of her . . . and you, Tammy. I kept hoping she'd calm down and return but she never did. Now perhaps we know why.'

'Was she friends with Lois Griffiths?'

'Aye. Her and that bairn of hers. He was about your age. Lois was adamant the treasure belonged to her family. She thought we knew the location. When I told her we didn't she turned her attention to your mother, saying all sorts, poisoning your mum's mind. Even then, she was a drinker.'

Gran passed a hand over her forehead.

'At that time, not knowing the location suited us Guardians fine. Our role was simply to keep it a secret, otherwise everyone and their dog would be scouring the Valley. Then there was the issue of who was entitled to the treasure; Catholics, Church of England, the descendants of the landed gentry who once owned parts of Arcana Valley — or the State. T'would have been a nightmare.'

I considered that. I was certain the situation was more clear-cut now. I recalled reading that a new Treasure Trove Act was being drafted for next year. Was that why Gran had agreed to co-operate with Darren Bruce in finding the hidden riches?

It appeared likely that Lois and friends had hoped to unearth this wealth first; she'd been pursuing this for quite a few years. The prospect of riches always did bring out the worst in people.

* * *

Sunday morning saw Kim arrive to collect me for the drive to the former residence of Lois Griffiths. She couldn't understand how we'd literally missed the boat, tracking down that canal craft of hers.

'What was it called?' she asked, as we turned from our drive way onto Misty River Road, heading up the dale.

'Mademoiselle A'Bor,' I replied, before bursting out laughing. 'Stupid me. I should have realised. The name sounds like Mademoiselle Arbor which means 'Miss Tree' in French. Mystery? Wonder why she chose that name?'

'Misty River was once called Mystery River, Tammy. Names change over time. According to the officers who went up to her place yesterday, it wasn't a pleasant experience. Maybe Rick was right calling it Spooky Valley. I've never been any further than your Gran's place, near the start.'

'Thinking about it, Kim, neither have I.'

The wide expanse of Misty River was on our right with the occasional white water of rapids disturbing the gentle flow downstream into the Calder. The sunny morning I'd woken up to had long since vanished as a phalanx of leaden clouds marched quickly across the sky towards us.

'Any further news on my favourite archer?' I enquired, recalling yesterday evening.

'Small-time idiot paid to scare you apparently. Well known to the local archery club as being easily led into stupid situations. He confessed everything once Rick began the interview. Rick admitted he'd used some ideas you taught him from the Good Cop, Bad Cop discussion with Mr Butterball. The poor archery kid wet himself. Said he was contacted by a woman on the phone and given fifty quid to frighten you. It transpires he never intended to shoot you — or so he says. In addition, he wants you arrested for GBH. No chance of that. He'll be taken to court tomorrow. We're going for attempted murder.'

'That's a sobering thought. A bit over the top, don't you think?'

'He shot arrows at you then threatened to use you as a bulls-eye, Tammy.'

I couldn't argue with that. It would

certainly send out a message to my enemy that the police weren't messing around.

As we drove, the Arcana Valley was narrowing, the steep, heavily-wooded sides almost menacing. We'd not seen another vehicle. This part of the Valley was sparsely populated, with good reason. Ahead a grey curtain of rain was almost upon us.

'Who'd possibly want to live up here?' Kim asked as the potholed Tarmac road changed to even more potholed gravel.

'Lord Nibberton the first, for one.' It was his former estate we were driving through, although now only the Manor House remained of his tyrannical legacy. Around the time when the canals had been built, he had been a powerful businessman, intent on using the canals to transport his quarried Millstone Grit sandstone throughout the country.

'Is that the guy that was so hated that he was nicknamed His Nibs by his disgruntled workers?'

I laughed again. 'I'd forgotten that. Do you think His Nibs will appreciate us wearing our work clothes to visit his posh home?'

'Not so posh now, according to the team from yesterday. And they saw it in the sunshine.'

Suddenly the car was awash with rain so heavy, it was difficult to see the road ahead.

There were huge gashes in the landscape where underpaid workers had quarried sandstone. They would have had to haul it out by horse and lorry. Using the river would have been impossible. No wonder Lord Nibberton had considered a branch line canal though the steep hills — a task which would have been an engineering nightmare.

'How far to Nibberton Manor, Tamara?'

'Not too far.' I looked at the rough map Gran had sketched. 'This isn't my idea of a fun day out. Even the trees give me the creeps.'

Instead of straight trunks, the ones either side were all gnarled and contorted as though infected with some crippling fungus or disease.

Through the mists of rain, a strange, turreted house appeared on the hillside ahead. It overlooked rapids of Misty River. The road wove back and forth as it snaked upwards, then levelled out as we pulled up to the front entrance.

★ ★ ★

I'd seen derelict houses before, but this one took the biscuit. What had once been a testament to power and prestige, with elegant Georgian architecture on three levels, it was a dilapidated shadow of its former self.

The Roman-style columns added absolutely nothing to the building. It had been built around the time of George III, according to the research I did last night. That monarch was also known as Mad King George. I think some of the madness had found its way here.

As we drove up the side of the imposing structure, I examined its sandstone walls, making a mental note of everything I could. Old habits were hard to break and I always believed there was no such thing as too much knowledge. A plastic pipe and heavy wooden doors in one part of the building looked well and truly out of place.

Moreover, I sensed an ambience here that seemed to seep into our car as well. There was something wrong with the land — maybe poisons saturating the soil, maybe something more mystical. Whatever it was, it gave me a sense of ill-ease.

'We'll have to make a dash for the front door. Apparently, it was open when the team came yesterday. Have you got our bag of goodies? There's no power, and it's hardly fine and sunny out here, so it'll be gloomy to say the least.'

We had flashlights, tools and cameras among other items.

'And if we're not alone?'

Kim tapped the shoulder holster under her anorak.

Outside, the torrential rain abated for a moment. With coats over our heads, we ran across the cobbled forecourt, up the stairs to the once-impressive sandstone façade and double doors. The symmetrically arranged sash windows were in dire need of maintenance. Clearly Lois Griffiths was not a DIY fanatic.

Just as we were about to cross the threshold, bells began to peal out from further up the dale.

Kim stared at me, perplexed.

'Didn't realise there was a church up there.'

I gave her a sober look back.

'There isn't. The road ends here. And we're at least ten miles from any village that way.'

The chimes subsided as quickly as they began, plunging us back into a rain-touched silence. Another eerie occurrence in Arcana Valley.

We made it inside to be greeted by huge, empty rooms with crumbling cornices and flaking ceilings. It was dark, too.

I tried a light switch, just in case. Nothing.

'Seems as though the place was cleared out some time ago. Yet this is her address?'

'On the electoral roll. Can't access council records for the last rate payment. They don't work on weekends,' Kim explained, donning forensics gloves.

'The place stinks,' I observed. It did outside, too. 'Reminds me of the smell where they process metal from ore. Maybe they used to do that here and the residue has contaminated the land. It would explain the deformed vegetation.'

We walked slowly through echoing rooms, kicking aside whatever items were scattered around on the floor in the search for anything of interest. The stolen mail, found yesterday, had apparently been from me, to me, or open cheques and money to others. Lois was undeniably a thief — and everything pointed to her being Darren Bruce's abductor.

'Kitchen?'

We headed in there. It was basic with running water, but there was nothing personal around.

'Where's the door to the basement?' I enquired, frustrated at our lack of progress.

Kim checked her team's notes. 'Apparently, there isn't one.'

The panes of one window were broken and water pooled across the floor. An oak leaf from the dying tree outside moved as our flashlights splayed across the water-covered tiles.

'OK. Nothing here,' Kim said. 'Let's try the bedrooms upstairs.'

'Wait, Kim. Listen . . .'

There was a faint sound of water flowing down. My torch beam focused on the leaf as it moved across what looked to be walnut parquet tiles.

'The water's going under that cupboard. Might be a secret door? Georgian houses usually did have basements. Well, according to the books I've read.'

'Glad you have this wide-ranging knowledge, Tammy. I'm sure you would have enjoyed that girl's magazine, Jackie, more though.'

'Oh, I don't know. Mum's idea of sex education was to give me a copy of the Kinsey reports, with a most enlightening book on genetic aspects of dairy cattle breeding in Uganda. After reading those, I had no interest in experimentation with acne-faced boys at school.'

We both tried to move the tall larder cupboard. Although it was empty, it wouldn't budge.

'Surely not a concealed release catch?' Kim asked.

I could see scratch marks on the floor where the cupboard hinged open. Brushing aside some cobwebs and a very irate spider, I pressed various panels on the wall. One sprang to the side as the cupboard shifted forward, then swung open to reveal a stairwell. The hinged door was on wheels and locked into place, wide open.

'After you,' Kim suggested.

We flashed our lights all around the cavernous hole below and, seeing no end to the stairs, I carefully edged forward.

'You do realise that this would be the part in the horror film when eerie, dramatic music would start up. At the very least you could hum something jolly like *Follow The Yellow Brick Road.*'

'True. You walk. I'll hum.'

I took one step down as Kim commenced the theme music from *Jaws.* I wasn't impressed.

There were only fifteen stone stairs, with a strong handrail. As soon as I reached the bottom, I fanned the torch around. More water was pooling in a far corner of the room with a glimmer of light coming from outside.

'Come on down,' I called. Kim joined me, being very careful on the wet, slippery stairs.

I explored the immediate area, deciding that the incongruous machine on one wall was my first port of call. A large rat scampered along the stone blocks before vanishing into a crevice.

'Aha. I know what that is,' I said of the device. We went across the vast basement to a shiny red and yellow generator. There was a half-full fuel can by its side.

Kim touched the machine.

'It's cold. Don't tell me you can start it up?'

I smiled. 'Basic Mechanics, October 1976.'

A quick investigation established there was some fuel in the generator and it was primed.

'Stand back, Kim.' I yanked the cord hard and was pleased to hear the newish machine begin chugging away immediately.

'Let there be light.' Crossing my fingers, I flipped a toggle switch and bulbs flooded the enclosed room with flickering illumination. The wiring leading from there suggested the rest of the house would light up too. Luckily, there was no rainwater near the wiring.

'Who's a clever bunny? You realise you've put my search team yesterday to shame. What's more, I suspect that pile of clothing over there might belong to Mr Bruce.'

She knelt, her face looking strange in the reflected light from the dampness nearby. It was getting cold, too.

Before placing the items in an evidence bag we'd brought, she confirmed our suspicions. She had notes and a photo with her. The torch flicked between them and the clothing.

'This is the jumper the poor man was wearing when he vanished.'

'We'd best clear out of here before you-know-who decides to come back.'

'No. We're not leaving. I'll call for back-up.'

She lifted her police radio but there was no signal. I tried my mobile; that was dead too.

From somewhere far away we heard the distinctive sound of rusty gears moving. Kim and I glanced at one another, the half-light in the basement mirroring our joint realisation. The door at the top of the stairs began to close, cutting out the dim daylight from the kitchen.

I heard Kim use a very unladylike word.

'Quick, Kim. Up the stairs. Jam the cupboard.'

We were halfway up when the entrance closed firmly with a loud, reverberating bang. A chilling vision of waking in darkness to hear the final nail being hammered into my coffin lid sprang to mind.

We'd been too slow.

No matter how hard we pushed or searched for another release lever, the solid oak structure refused to budge.

'Shame they didn't have MFI back

when this kitchen was done. Would have made escaping a lot easier,' I observed, wiping the perspiration from my brow.

There was obviously some ancient timing device set to reseal the hidden entrance after some minutes. I could see the pulleys and chain linkages, now I knew what to look for. Whoever had set it up, possibly Lord Nibberton himself, wanted his hidden entrance to this basement kept hush-hush.

But why? It was simply a basement.

At that moment the generator spluttered then gave two final coughs and a hiccup before dying altogether. We were plunged into darkness once more. I turned on my torch, illuminating Kim's very concerned expression.

'Any suggestions about what do we do now, Tammy? It'll be hours before my colleagues realise we're missing.'

I leaned back against the basement wall and gave Kim a small chocolate bar from our holdall bag, before opening one myself. I prayed I was right in my reasoning — otherwise we were in for a long, uncomfortable wait.

'Time for Plan B, Detective Inspector Byrne. I'm afraid it's going to be messy though. We're both going to need a long, hot shower afterwards.'

I led her down the stairs before shining my torch at the far corner of the basement.

She was flabbergasted.

'You have got to be kidding me, Tammy. You don't expect me to climb through that.'

I tucked in my shirt, then my jeans into my socks, before pulling my hair back in a ponytail.

'Looks like me first again.'

9

A plastic pipe snaked along the wall from the generator. It was to remove the toxic exhaust fumes and carbon monoxide. To use the generator without it would have had dreadful consequences for anyone down here, even with the door to the kitchen open.

From the floor, it turned at ninety degrees, ascending to the ceiling then outside through a doorway once used to dump coal in here. There was a glimmer of light from the wooden doors to the outside. That's how I proposed we escape this dungeon. The only problem was . . . we'd have to scramble up a hill of damp black coal.

'Why don't you climb out, Tammy, then open the hidden door at the top of the stairs?' Kim suggested. 'I've just had my hair done.'

'Fair enough. But you'll be in my

debt forever and a day.'

Kim trained her flashlight on me as I started to clamber up the rain-soaked coal slope. My journey consisted of one step upwards and a long back. It was a good thing the doors were only ten feet up. I'd noticed them and the exhaust pipe as we'd driven up.

'How are you going, Tammy?' I heard Kim call out. By that time, I was too tired to use the words I wanted to.

'Tickety-boo,' I spluttered as a cloud of damp coal dust enveloped me.

'Well. It was your idea, kid. You're almost there. Those doors look fairly rotten.'

Gasping, I reached up to grab the side of the coal chute, then pushed one door outwards as far as I could. It swung back and a gust of rain almost dislodged me from my precarious perch.

Quickly I dragged myself out and stood up to let the torrential rain at least wash some of the accumulated gunge from me. It helped a bit.

After releasing Kim, she made a suggestion that I have a shower in the Manor House bathroom. I gave it a miss. I'd had my fill of this place. However, Kim wasn't finished with her helpful suggestions. I was about to get into the police car when she politely requested that I put some plastic sheeting from her boot over the fabric-covered seat.

The trip back was uncomfortable. There was lots of squelching, and anger at having been trapped down there. Still, we had found additional evidence to further implicate the evil Lois Griffiths.

★ ★ ★

Once home, I was about to head for the shower when Gran caught sight of me.

'No way, Tammy. You look as bad as you did when you were covered in mud from a fight with one of the other kiddies. I'll hose you off outside. What is it?'

'Coal gunge, Gran. And it wasn't my fault this time either.'

'Outside, sweetheart. I'll get the hose. Get those clothes off first.'

Feeling quite self-conscious, I did as Gran suggested. This part of the garden was well enclosed. I opted to keep my undies on but it was obvious they would never come clean again. A pity. They were some of my favourites.

'Ready?'

I nodded as a stream of tepid water struck me. I began cleaning as much of the muck off my skin as I could.

'You missed a bit!' Kim yelled in glee from the sidelines.

It took twenty minutes under the shower before I felt I was free of the last speck of blackness. Donning some fresh clothes, I returned to Amanda and Gran who were preparing a hot meal for lunch.

Kim asked that the three of us continue searching the family records for whatever Darren had been after, as well as working on deciphering the six cryptic notes that Cyril had seen fit to send to my grandparents.

While we busied ourselves, Amanda told me of Kim's plans back at the station. She was intent on checking out every aspect of Lois Griffiths' life; her history, relatives, and why she was living in that creepy Manor House. In short, she wanted to find out exactly who she was dealing with.

That meant her team digging around, possibly ruffling a few feathers in the process. Dotty had worked with her, so she might have some insight so she was Kim's first port of call.

I waited until we'd finished lunch and tidied up before asking Amanda about Darren.

'We found some personal items of Darren's at the Manor House. Combined with the fact that Darren's case was planted in Gran's car, it seems certain that his disappearance is tied up with this huge mess.'

'Kim told us about your adventures this morning. As for Darren, he's simply an investigator.'

I thought about that.

'It seems unlikely Lois would need him this long for whatever she's doing, presumably fortune hunting. Anything special about him at all?'

'He's a Libran, has a wife and two children, likes chilli. Plays footie at the weekends as well as caving.'

'Caving?'

'Bit of an expert, apparently. There are no caves around here that I know of, though. Do you, Mum?' she asked Gran.

Gran wiped her hands on her apron.

'Don't believe so. Even though that's the ancient story about the hiding place. I suppose it makes sense to put valuables in a place that's unknown, even to the locals.'

Amanda continued. 'Which brings me back to something Tammy and I discovered before any of Darren's possessions were found, Mum. We found a newspaper cutting about Darren Bruce disappearing and wondered why you kept it. Was it because Darren came from the same town I live in?'

'Heavens no, Amanda. I kept it because I recollect young Darren from when he was a bairn. He lived here in the Valley.'

Amanda looked so shocked, I feared that she might go into labour.

'I investigated him going missing. How could I possibly have bypassed that?'

'Oh, he weren't here long, Amanda. A year, maybe two. Lived up t'other end.'

'Not up near Nibberton's home?' I asked.

'Close by, I suppose. Must be . . . oh, twenty years since. Gramps had suffered his first heart attack. Darren's dad came to the hospital to visit. Pleasant fella, from what I remember. He used to go caving, too.'

We sat down in the lounge. The picture was at last beginning to take shape. If Lois had found out from Cyril about buried or hidden treasure, she might have been searching for it all these years. Having also heard about the Guardians who might stop her, she seemed to have devised a long-term scheme to make certain her quiet investigating wouldn't be noticed.

I believed she'd taken me and infected me with this local disease, the Fairy Touch, then she'd convinced my mother to keep me away from Arcana Valley. Furthermore, I suspected that she'd either poisoned my mum's mind, alienating her or given her money to disappear.

Any correspondence between us had been intercepted so that I was never able to learn about my heritage as a protector of this Reformation cache of jewels and money that was once secreted in the area by the Knights Hospitaller.

Gramps wasn't well; Mum had forsaken her heritage, which left me as the only obstacle in Lois' decade-long search. No wonder I'd been threatened the moment I'd arrived back here.

It now appeared to be a race between our family, along with Kim, versus malevolent Lois and her unnamed henchman.

I sensed that the jumbled cryptic letters from Cyril that Gran had kept contained some clues about where to search. Logic didn't suggest I was right, yet some inner sixth sense told me I was.

I'd never believed in Extra Sensory Perception or ghosts and fairies before — yet, remembering those spectral voices down by Tammy's Bridge, it had started me thinking. Maybe I did have the ability to perceive the truth hidden behind hundreds of lies. Despite everything I'd been told and felt about myself these past eleven years, maybe I was special, in some mysterious way.

Gran insisted on continuing to nurse me, carefully applying the plant extracts that she maintained would restore my health. Given how well I now felt, I didn't complain. Even the smell of the yellow and red paste didn't upset me any longer. I trusted her implicitly.

★ ★ ★

I gave Amanda and Gran the handwritten page and sat them together on the settee. I had memorised each message and sat opposite them. No alcohol; we needed clear heads. Amanda volunteered to make notes.

Gran read the notes out in their entirety. I'd given each of them a number.

1. Remember the promise, Mildred Hathaway.

2. Gold coins, silver coins, shiny jewels and treasure. Hidden by the church men, discovered at my leisure.

3. When 'tis silin', off bleggin', eyen the goosegogs, thissen.

4. Today's the day Teddy has his picnic.

5. Ring a ring a rosie.

6. Who's afraid of the big, bad wolf? Vervain won't save her now.

'Initial thoughts, anyone?'

I'd heard that brainstorming was an effective method of solving problems although it was a new experience. Still, three generations of our special family tackling a puzzle together was something to savour even if we achieved nothing.

'We've already decided that numbers one and two are associated with Cyril trying to get your attention about discovering the treasure hoard,' Amanda stated.

Gran was clearly in some pain from the arthritis yet she was determined to add her thoughts. She was doing well considering her age. Possibly it was the perfect pick-me-up for her; feeling useful once more. She brushed back a strand of silvery hair from her glasses.

'That don't mean that that's the only significance they have. The Fairy Touch and 'ring a ring of rosie' are connected too.'

I had to know. 'Gran. Could you translate number three? I failed Yorkshirish at school.'

Gran chuckled. 'T'ain't difficult, my girl. You know what goosegogs are, don't you?'

I recalled her telling me. 'Gooseberries. What about the rest?'

'Literally it means *when it's pouring down and you're foraging, looking for gooseberries, yourself.* Eyen is an ancient word for eyes using an old English plural that is still around in words like children and oxen.'

I examined Amanda's puzzled face. She shifted around to get comfortable before deciding that it would be better for her and the baby to stand for a while.

'Mum. Tammy and I accept your translation, however it's clear as mud to us. Does it mean anything to you?'

'Cyril, the others and I used to pick gooseberries. One boy, Chris, used to love eating them off the bush. He allus was a strange 'un. But no, there's nothing special there except it's the only message written in dialect.'

'Almost like a secret code only some

people would understand,' I mused aloud. 'OK. That one's a puzzle. What about number four? Do you know anything about a boy named Teddy or Edward? And what's this about a picnic?'

'We used to have picnics all the time, our little gang. Don't recollect anyone called Teddy though, Tammy.'

Amanda suggested. 'What about the song that line is from? *The Teddy Bear's Picnic.*'

I added my thoughts to the discussion. 'Lyrics were written in 1930 by an Englishman to accompany the music written by an American called *The Teddy Bear Two-Step.*'

Gran and Amanda stared at me in wonder.

'Don't you get tired of being so clever, Tammy?' was Amanda's comment.

'Remembering stuff isn't clever, Auntie. It's using that knowledge that's important.'

'Nevertheless, I'm really signing you

up for my future pub-quiz team. You'll be perfect.'

We all knew the lyrics. Gran would have been twelve or thirteen when the song came out. It had been very popular. The song was about teddies having a picnic in the woods and if you wanted to see them, you'd best be in disguise. Again, it didn't seem to mean anything more to Gran than being a popular song from her childhood.

'We're not getting anywhere with this,' Amanda declared, frustrated. 'Would you mind if I had a lie down for an hour or so?'

'Of course not,' we both told her. I realised she was missing Paul. He was due back from Berlin in a few days.

Once she'd gone, Gran and I moved onto number six. *Who's afraid of the big, bad wolf?*

'This song came out in 1933. It was in a Disney cartoon about the *Three Little Pigs*.'

'I remember it, Tammy. I had left the group by then and before you ask, there weren't no wolves around here. Another dead end. Cyril must have been ... well, his mind must have been going, unfortunately. As for vervain, it's just a herb. I don't use it in curing the Fairy Touch and neither did Mum. Vervain is used for anxiety. You might know it as Holy Herb or Pigeonweed. Lots of names and uses. There are only a few places it exists in the Valley.'

Our brainstorming had been less than spectacular. There was a message in there, and I sensed it was important. However it was also elusive.

* * *

The remainder of the day and evening was thankfully uneventful. I made a list of what I wanted to search for in the Manchester Library and settled down to sleep. I'd excused myself early, leaving Amanda and Gran enjoying memories from photo albums back when she was a child.

I was in my old room. It was

strangely comforting. As the rain began again, softly pitter-pattering on the window, I drifted off to sleep.

Not much later I heard a voice; a male one. Instantly I was awake, fumbling for my dressing gown and a cricket bat I'd found and put in my bedroom. I could hear Amanda's voice too.

Damn. More trouble. Gingerly I opened the door. The voices were in Amanda's room further down the lino-floored corridor. They weren't raised so I couldn't make out what was being said, but a stranger in the house meant one thing as far as I was concerned — Tammy to the rescue.

I crept up to the door in my slippers and, brandishing the bat, threw the door open.

Amanda and the man in bed with her stared at me in surprise before my aunt gently said, 'Tammy. You can put the bat down. This is my husband, Paul.'

10

Talk about embarrassing. I put the cricket bat down.

'Pleased to meet you, Paul,' I said, trying not to look at the two of them in bed together.

'And you, Tammy,' he replied.

'I'll . . . see you in the morning.' I backed out of the room and returned to my bedroom wondering if I'd be traumatised for life.

Over breakfast, it was explained how Paul had chosen to return home on an earlier flight and had come here as a surprise. He had rung Amanda on her mobile when stopped at the gate by an officer and was allowed inside after that. I'd been asleep, so they decided not to wake me. In the end, it didn't matter.

I was hoping for a lift to the station at Hebden to get the train to Manchester's Victoria Station but with Paul's arrival, I felt guilty about expecting anyone to taxi me around. Once I did pluck up the courage to ask, Amanda surprised me by saying no, that they had other plans.

I was disappointed and it must have shown.

Amanda giggled. 'Cheer up, sourpuss. Rick's collecting you and driving you down the whole way. Imagine, an hour with him all alone. Whatever will you do?'

'Well — certainly not what you and Paul were doing when I burst in.'

Gran's eyes widened. I'd put my foot in it again.

Amanda gave me a wink.

'Relax, Mum,' she said to my gran. 'We were just kissing — weren't we, Tammy?'

Rick arrived at ten with an update. Lois and her canal boat were still nowhere to be found. It was yet another conundrum on the long list.

'I gather I'm getting a lift to Manchester, Rick. Police business — or do you just fancy a day out with me?'

'Police business, Tammy. I'm research-ing Lois Griffiths. She lived around Manchester for a long time before moving here a dozen years ago. I could do it on the phone, but there are some security issues. You don't mind going with me?'

'Of course not. As long as we're not using that Matchbox car of yours?'

'You don't like Bertie?' He laughed, pushing his hair back from his eyes. I stared.

'Bertie the Beetle?' he elaborated.

'Naming your car, Rick? Thought you were a real man. Next you'll be saying you play tiddlywinks.'

'Champion for North West England, three years in a row. I have a gold medal I wear under my shirt. Want to see it?'

It was my turn to laugh.

'You're as mad as me, DS Turpin. Shall we get going, then? If we have time, I'd like to collect post from my home plus some paperwork for my job.

I can do it up here if I use Amanda's computer.'

We'd been having some coffee in the empty kitchen but now Amanda walked in.

'Tammy. Did I just hear you invite this young man around to your place?' she asked.

'No. It's just that — ' I began.

'Relax, Tammy. I'm teasing. You're an adult. You don't need to explain your actions, either of you.'

This time it was Rick who blushed first.

'DI Lightfield. I would never dream of behaving inappropriately with your niece, at least until this whole Annabelle and Lois affair is all solved — '

'When you'll behave as inappropriately as you like?' Amanda grinned and left the room.

Rick was cringeing.

'I didn't mean that, Tammy.'

I took his hand as I grabbed my handbag and led him to the front door, where I donned my borrowed sun-glasses.

'Don't apologise, DS Turpin. We're as bad as one another for saying and doing the wrong thing. Let me tell you about me walking in on Amanda and her husband, last night . . . '

★ ★ ★

The police car Rick drove was a vast improvement on his VW Beetle. And it was clean inside. The plan for our trip was for me to research the history of Arcana Valley, particularly the part of the Rochdale Canal that flowed through Hebden. I was certain there was a connection between the canal, Lord Nibberton (His Nibs) and his manor house where Lois and her son had lived.

Rick was investigating Lois and her family in more detail. He told me she had a criminal record.

We turned at Sowerby Bridge intending to join the M62 just past Ripponden, then turn off around Oldham to go through the suburbs into Manchester. The weather was cloudy and without rain. That was a good thing. Driving over the Moors in bad weather wasn't much fun.

I had a licence but no car at the moment. Living in the centre of Manchester, I had my pick of public transport, and the converted mill where my apartment was didn't have parking anyway.

Even now, the Moors were bleak. Gone was the lush vegetation in Arcana Valley.

'Tell me about yourself, Rick. I want to find out what's behind that baby-face of yours.'

With his looks, he could have been the lead singer with a boy band. Not one to pussyfoot around, I decided to go for the jugular.

'So — why are you unattached?'

I'd mentally eliminated the most obvious ones. He didn't have bad breath; no acne; he had a fine sense of humour and was easy to talk to without being egotistical.

'Truth?'

'Yes, please.'

'I gather you had parent problems. Same with me. I grew up seeing the worst aspects of marriage and relationships. Don't get me wrong, my parents loved me. It was each other they couldn't stand. Divorce was out of the question so they've spent the past twenty-seven years hating one another. Now they live in different parts of the same house. I visit them separately. It was a waste of both their lives.'

'So you left home to concentrate on your career with the police? Makes sense. I just can't believe I'm the first girl you've fancied.'

'Of course you're not. There was that redhead in primary school and Miss Tyler, my French teacher when I was fourteen. Also, a long list of disastrous short-term relationships. To be honest, I'm not easy to live with. Plus, I'm a cop. We tend to be a moody lot, dealing with the scum who prey on innocent people. We're immersed in the worst that society has to offer, and it drags us down at times. Not many women like cops.'

'I do,' I confessed. 'I've seen the good they can do. Kim finding me wandering around Hebden in a daze all those years ago, the older Sergeant who spent hours with me after telling me my parents were both dead — even that constable saving me from that mad archer on Saturday.'

'Yeah, Big Mac. Steve MacDonald. There's something about him that isn't right, though. He and I have had a few words in the past.'

We turned down the slip road at junction twenty-two near the highest point of any English motorway. From an almost empty single lane road, we were immersed in a mad whirl of trucks, cars and buses moving at the speed limit and faster. I gritted my teeth. Motorway driving always terrified me, partly because of the scene after my parents' car crashed into the barrier. The TV coverage gave me nightmares for a week.

'You OK, Tammy?'

Rick wove effortlessly into the bedlam of traffic, smoothly and safely changing lanes so that we were in the middle.

'Don't like motorways,' I told him, releasing my grip on the arm rest a little.

'I'm a fully trained tactical pursuit driver, Tammy. When I was in uniform, I drove high-speed cars. Even with idiots all around us who should never be allowed behind a wheel, you're safe with me.'

It wasn't conceit, simply a statement of fact. His eyes were constantly searching for potential problems and checking the rear view mirror. Rick was in control and, unlike drivers in *The Bill* who looked over to their passengers all the time, Rick was focused.

He wore a bright, swirly-pattened tie over his white short-sleeved shirt, making me feel underdressed in a loose blouse and cream jeans.

'What about yourself, Miss Tammy? You mentioned this KFC guy. Kyle. No regrets about him not being with him any longer?'

I thought about Kyle for a moment. His light brown hair was always short and although he had a boyish face that some girls would fall in love with, his continual surly expression put me off from day one. He'd appeared in my life one afternoon in a park, striking up a friendly conversation with me.

I'd never encouraged him, not even a kiss, yet he seemed to be everywhere from that day on; on the bus, in my local supermarket. He'd always wanted to chat and, to begin with, I guess I'd been flattered. After all, boys had given me a wide berth at school.

The day he'd turned up at my front door was the day I decided enough was enough and told him. Although he'd never come around again, he seemed to still be wherever I was. Maybe it was what others called stalking, yet he'd not threatened me so I'd not approached the police. I'd moved to Manchester a few weeks later and that was that.

'We were never together. I guess he was the closest I've ever had to a friend who was a boy but kisses and cuddles were never on my agenda. Possibly he wanted more? Who knows? Looking back at how I was just a few days ago, I never felt good enough to have anyone in my life. That Touch thing.

'But even before Gran started treating me, I thought there was an attraction between you and me . . . sort of like soulmates. I hope you feel the same way — otherwise I've screwed up again, over-sharing my feelings.'

'You haven't 'screwed up', as you put it, Tammy. While I still have no idea what the real Tammy Jordan is like after these past few days, I'm looking forward to finding out.'

★　★　★

209

Within another half hour we were approaching Manchester. I wanted to go to the main library in St Peter's Square whereas Rick was headed to Chester House, a mile or so outside the centre.

He dropped me off with the promise to keep in touch on our mobiles to arrange collection later on. I figured two hours should have been sufficient.

In the end it was closer to three.

My research was geared around the canal plans and maps drawn up hundreds of years earlier. Lord Nibberton was heavily involved in the finance and, naturally, the planning of the route. He'd originally wanted the Rochdale Canal to bypass Hebden and go through Arcana Valley. According to records, he didn't have a clue about the logistics of canals and steep hills. His preferred route would have necessitated fifty-seven locks over a sixteen-mile stretch. The route through Hebden was tricky enough, with eighteen locks in total between over ten miles.

I discovered that His Nibs did build some feeder canals around 1800, through some very strange places, some of which made no sense to me at all. I wondered if they were still there, hidden from the tourists and canal enthusiasts who thought they knew it all. Could Lois Griffiths and her boat have hidden in one of them?

As for Lord Nibberton himself and his eccentric Manor House, the information in the library was very sketchy. There was a portrait of the old goat, resplendent in his finery. He wore a sneer, probably showing his contempt for the unfortunate artist painting his Lordship's likeness.

Contemporary accounts of him indicated he was a cruel, chauvinistic sadist. Ugly, too. There was something familiar about his eyes, though I couldn't think what.

I made copies of the parts I thought pertinent to the investigation. Did His Nibs have information about the long-concealed riches and had he tried to find it? I doubted it. He'd apparently died of some foul disease, although his body was never found. His children had disowned him and, from all accounts, he went bust when the railway came to town, superseding the slower canal boats.

★ ★ ★

I went outside to wait for Rick in his unmarked police car. It was balmy, noisy and busy, being lunchtime. Rather than eat at one of the many restaurants or cafes nearby, I decided we could grab a bite in my apartment overlooking the canal.

The vaulted ceilings of the former warehouse were the first thing that had appealed to me when I'd come to buy it last year. With the insurance money from the deaths of my parents, I was able to scrape up enough for a deposit. I'd been lucky.

My apartment was only two bed-rooms, yet it was now valued by the developer at twenty thousand pounds more than I paid. It seemed that it was becoming trendy to live in the centre of our city. They'd even restored the canal.

Rick pulled into a parking spot opposite where I was standing. I hurried across.

'How did you get on?' he asked as I belted up.

'Enlightening. You?'

'Super enlightening. Where are we going now?'

'My place for lunch and comparing notes. Next right, then second on the left. I'll guide you. There's no parking in the building but there's pay parking opposite.'

We were there in a couple of minutes; the advantages of an inner-city address. The new Metro-Link tram system passed by not far away.

There were quite a few people around as we pulled up. Rick took a long look around as we got out. I'd grabbed some milk and salad from a shop near the library, so had my hands full with that, my copied notes and paperwork. Rick had an attaché case.

'Impressive digs, Tammy. Is the canal on the other side of the building?'

I nodded. 'Mod cons, security door plus a gym in the basement. Not that I use it.'

Rick stopped and knelt down as we approached the front entrance.

'Loose shoe lace. You go on. I'll catch you up.'

I unlocked the door, by which time Rick was back by my side. 'No concierge?' he joked, admiring the impressive foyer.

We took the lift to the top floor before walking down the wide corridor to my place.

In a way it was good to be back here, among the possessions that were mine and had meant so much. In the week I'd been up at Gran's, my life had changed in so many ways. I'd noticed it even wandering around the streets of Manchester; a sense of confidence, almost power. I wasn't the timid, frightened person I'd been when I left.

Last week this had been my sanctuary, my safe place where I could watch passers-by on the canal from up above. Now, I felt I wanted to be out there with people — not hiding from them.

Rick was the first man I'd invited here. It felt good. I was sure he'd approve of my modern furniture and fabrics but more than that, I hoped he'd approve of me and my choices. He did.

'Impressive set-up, Tammy. And that painting. Is that a Ruldolph Rann print? I love his work. Limited edition too. That must have set you back.'

'I did some work for him a year or so back when I was just starting out. It was a gift. Nice guy. We still keep in touch.'

The bedroom door was open. Fortunately, the bed was made. Although I hadn't been expecting visitors when I left, I didn't want Rick thinking I was an untidy slob. I offered him a coffee but just as the kettle boiled, he called out, 'Sorry. Left a file in the car. I'll just be a mo. OK to take your door keys?'

'Yeah. I'll make a start on lunch. Don't be long. We have a lot to discuss.'

It was only after he left that my mind caught up with an inconsistency I must have noticed. He'd bent down to tie his laces outside, though he was in fact wearing slip-on leather shoes. Puzzled, I wandered through into my second bedroom which had a view of the parking lot.

I peered down at his car, waiting for him to return. Instead I watched as it backed up, then drove to the exit barrier before disappearing back towards the city centre.

'What the hell?'

It didn't make sense. Worse still, he had my keys. Where was he going? Thinking about calling his mobile, I stopped when I saw it on the table, next to the police files he'd brought.

'Maybe he's gone back to Chester House?' I wondered aloud. There wasn't much I could do and being certain he wouldn't be that long, I returned to the kitchen.

It was only a few minutes later, that the doorbell buzzed. The video security camera was just for the entrance foyer to the building so I assumed Rick might be struggling with the state-of-the-art deadlock on my apartment.

Opening the door, I began to ask Rick what he was playing at.

The trouble was, it wasn't Rick standing there. It was my so-called ex, Kyle — surly as ever.

'Surprise, Tammy.' He put his foot in the door opening before I could slam it closed. Then he calmly pushed the door ajar and shoved me to one side against a wall.

His eyes narrowed as he wiped the back of his hand across his mouth.

11

What are you doing, Kyle? Get out of here this instant.'

Calmly he walked over and sat down on a settee, sprawling as though he owned the place.

'Hmmm. Great joint you've got here. And you're making some lunch for me.'

I was furious. There was no way I could force him to leave. Instead I picked up my mobile and dialled 999. Before I could speak, he'd jumped up and smashed my phone on the tiled floor.

'That wasn't very friendly of you, Tammy. And don't go expecting that bloke you're with to come back. I just watched him drive off. Heard him talking to someone on his phone saying he was going to Liverpool. So, it's you and your old mate, Rooster. Just like old times.'

What he was saying made no sense. Not only was Rick's phone on the table — hidden by the salad bowl and condiments — but also there was absolutely no call for him to drive off to Liverpool.

I began to understand what Rick was really doing. Suddenly I felt much better.

'I'm very disappointed in you, Tammy. Leaving me like that without any forwarding address. Anyone would think you didn't want to see me again. Naughty girl. You and me, we're made for one another. I've been in love with you since I first saw you back in Yorkshire. Course you were only a kid back then like me, but I realised right away you were the one for me.'

'Kyle — I don't love you. Actually, I don't even like you.'

'Don't matter. If I love you, that's what counts. I loved you even when you were poorly, like.'

I couldn't believe what he was saying. I never realised he'd met me when I was a girl. It was his arrogant attitude, dismissing any opinions I might have about a loving relationship, that shocked me the most. Clearly, he had been stalking me long before our first 'accidental' meeting as adults.

If I'd known then what I now knew, I would never have spoken to him. How stupid was I? On reflection, I'd made some serious mistakes.

At that moment, Rick entered from the hallway. Although Kyle had locked the door, Rick had my keys.

'You OK, Tammy?' Rick's voice was much deeper than that of my unwanted intruder.

Relieved as anything, I ran to him, stubbing my toe on the remnants of my phone.

'Thank goodness, Rick. It's . . . '

'Kyle Francis Costello. Age twenty-five. Also known as Rooster because of his KFC connection. Funny thing that, Tammy. KFC deal with chickens, not roosters — so this waste of space should be using a different nickname altogether.'

Kyle came forward, aggressively. Rick ignored his posturing.

'But . . . but . . . but . . . ' Kyle began before Rick turned to me laughing.

'Hear that, Tammy? 'Bok . . . bok . . . bok'. Just like a chicken.'

Kyle's face became redder as he clenched both fists.

'I'll sort you out, mate. Good and proper.'

Rick's response changed from jovial to menacing as he faced Kyle and moved his feet apart. Even then, he failed to lift his open hands.

'What are you going to do, Mr Chicken? Herb and spice me to death?'

Kyle backed down at that, both humiliated by Rick's cutting words as well as by the supreme confidence exuded by the man by my side.

'Whoever you are, mate, you got no business here. Tammy's my girlfriend. Anyway, I saw you drive off. Liverpool, you said.'

'I'm a policeman, Kyle. I've found out all about you. Your criminal record

— which is very pathetic, I must admit — and who your mother is. Now, apart from breaking your conditions for your suspended sentence, I can arrest you for your actions today.'

'What actions, copper?'

Rick nodded to the shattered phone on the floor. 'Criminal damage. Breaking and entering. Threatening behaviour to Miss Jordan here . . . Shall I go on?'

'I didn't break in here. My girlfriend let me in.' Kyle spat out his angry words. I made a mental note to disinfect the floor later.

'I watched you break the glass downstairs, you idiot. Took some pretty photos, too. You were lurking around outside when Miss Jordan and I were entering. Recognised you from your mug shots on our files.'

That's when Rick had pretended to re-tie his non-existent shoe lace. Going outside and acting as if he was going to drive to Liverpool was all a ploy to allow Kyle to do whatever he planned.

Rick removed a set of handcuffs from

his back trouser pocket.

Realising he was in serious trouble, Kyle surprised us both by going into psycho mode again. He put his right hand into his own pocket then held up a vial of some powder.

'Think you're so clever, copper? Do you? Well, think on this.'

With that he hurled the glass vial at the tiles causing a cloud of pungent grey powder to envelop us all. I took an involuntary breath and my entire body went limp.

The last thing I recall seeing before I passed out was Rick falling hard against a chair which collapsed, sending him crashing onto the worktop. Kyle was running out of the door. The clock behind them said twelve minutes past two.

When I opened my eyes, it was nineteen minutes past two. My head was so groggy.

'Rick!' My speech was slurred. I struggled to sit up. 'RICKKK!'

He didn't move. That powder was all around us and on our clothing and hair.

Every time I moved it flew into the air again.

Straining with effort, I pulled myself up until I was standing. It was two twenty-three.

Must be the dust, I reasoned. It had made us sleepy. Why wasn't Rick stirring?

Then I recalled the smell. I'd been exposed to it before. There was darkness . . . and the sound of lapping water . . . blue and twinkling like the stars.

I'd been twelve when I'd disappeared: My mind was struggling to focus. Maybe I had some sort of resistance to it? One thing was certain. I had to get Rick away from the powder.

There was no possibility of lifting his dead weight. He must be twelve stone or more.

Grabbing his legs, I pulled him little by little over to the kitchen area. Lord, he was heavy; more than I thought. The dust was still all over him. I tried to brush it off yet it settled on him once again.

Think, you stupid woman, I told myself.

Ring someone? No. Too slow. I hoped my moving him hadn't done harm. I hadn't been thinking straight.

Vacuum cleaner, I thought with one of those Eureka moments. I could use the attachments.

It took longer than usual to set it up. The cleaner was one of those with allergen filters. I'd reasoned that would help with my occasional asthma attacks which I now suspected were from the Touch. However fine the dust was, the cleaner could handle it.

'What did you do this afternoon, Tammy?' I could imagine Amanda asking later.

'Nothing much. A bit of cleaning. I spent ages vacuuming some sleeping powder from a charismatic young policeman who was lying on my kitchen floor. You wouldn't believe how awkward it was, getting into those hard-to-reach places.'

It took a while, clearing as much of

the horrible grey stuff as I could. And the smell . . .

I'd undone his shirt, which was covered with the dust. I was moving the upholstery brush through his hair when Rick suddenly stirred.

'What the . . . ?' he demanded, sitting up a bit.

'Thank goodness. Are you OK?'

'Sore as anything. What are you doing, Tammy?'

'Getting the sleeping powder off you. Probably ruined my cleaner but you're worth it.'

As he pulled himself to his feet, a bit more dust flew into the air. He staggered and I had to support him from falling again.

'Whoa. Dizzy.'

'Need to get that. Hold onto the chair and I'll give your back a clean.'

I switched the machine back on and did a very professional job with the brush. He only complained once about it tickling. Once I was finished, he could stand unaided. He shrugged off his open shirt and his vest.

'Don't think there's anything broken,' he announced after gentle prodding all around. His slurred speech was gone but the bruises where he'd struck the furniture were already quite pronounced. Pity I didn't have any Arnica cream. Gran had told me it was good for bruises.

'What are you staring at Tammy?'

'You. You're quite hairy. Not like I imagined.'

Damn. Another foot in mouth situation. I chewed my lip.

Gingerly he replaced his vest and shirt. When I offered to help him, he politely declined.

'I can dress myself, thanks. Have you phoned anyone? Police? Ambulance?'

I shook my head.

'Fair enough. I'll contact Chester House to get an APB out on Kyle.' All Points Bulletin, I recalled from *The Bill*. 'He's probably gone to ground. We'll skip getting bogged down with the local hospitals. Your gran can sort me out. She was a doctor, you know. Can you drive us there?'

'Yes. But not on the motorway. You'll have to navigate a bit. Are you up to it?'

He nodded, wincing from the pain.

'I'm sorry, Rick. I had no idea how he found me or that he was like that. You tried to help me and . . . I'm really sorry.'

He moved over to gently embrace me.

'Not your fault, pretty woman.' He kissed me on my forehead, then drew back.

I picked up the vacuum cleaner canister to take to Gran. I suspected it was one of those strange plant chemicals and she might recognise it.

Intuitively Rick realised what I was doing.

'Rick. Before we go. You recognised Kyle from his mugshot, but why would you be investigating him? He was simply some maniac who fancied me. Also, you told him you knew who his mother was. Care to explain?'

'Not that hard to work out Lois

228

Griffiths? Kyle Costello? Mother and son. Those two have been manipulating your life for a long time.'

I gasped, feeling a different kind of giddy as the shock settled in. What the hell did this wicked family want with me? Whatever it was, I was now more determined than ever to make them pay.

* * *

I used to have a car, so I wasn't a total novice to driving. The simple fact was that I didn't like motorways.

Rick was clearly uncomfortable as he fastened his seat belt. We headed up towards Oldham Road. From Oldham we'd climb up onto the Saddleworth Moors and into Yorkshire, home of Yorkie bars, decent tea bags and strange speaking ex-cricket players turned television commentators. Already I was feeling that was more my home than Lancashire. I had brought my mail and enough work to keep me busy (and paid) for a few weeks.

Although we were both quite hungry, we decided to avoid the KFC drive-through as it had very bad connotations. Instead we opted for fish burgers from the opposition, plus shakes. It gave us a chance to swap our respective discoveries, although topping the news about Lois and Kyle being related would take some doing.

'Me first,' I said. 'Lord Nibberton built a number of private canal paths that join up with the main one. Funny thing is, there's no mention of them on the maps today.'

I showed Rick the maps and plans.

'Hmm. I've jogged along that towpath dozens of times. Another canal branching off would be hard to miss. Very curious. Any idea why?'

'Not yet. The other thing was that he was mining metal ore, illegally.'

'That would explain the contaminated soil up that end of the Valley,' Rick said.

I recalled the deformed vegetation.

And yet, downstream there wasn't a problem. Another mystery.

'Tell me, Mr Detective. What else did you discover about Lois and family? Anything juicy?'

Rick winced again as he stretched. He pointed to the folders he had taken from his attaché case.

'Lois and Kyle were both living in the Manor House because they're the only relatives of Lord Nibberton. They both have records for various crimes. Can't understand how Lois got her job in the Post Office. No doubt there'll be some questions asked about that.'

Pieces were beginning to come together in this complex jigsaw. I hoped that what I'd discovered would join another few bits together.

First things first, though. We needed to get back to Gran's place for her to do some of her miracle ministrations on Rick's injuries. In addition, it was almost time for another session for me. There was no way I was doing anything to jeopardise my own recovery. Being healthy was so much better than the shadow that used to be me. Besides, Gran had a great deal to teach me about using plants to heal with homoeopathy.

Rick having rung ahead on his mobile, Kim was at Gran's old house when we pulled up. He made his own way inside where they were all waiting.

I'd brought the vacuum cleaner canister as well as all the paperwork. Following Rick, I could see he was struggling to walk upright but, being a typical man, he refused my assistance.

He insisted on being treated in front of everyone so that we all were brought up to date as quickly as possible. There was Amanda, Paul, Kim and, of course, Gran.

'Right young man. Strip off. Top half only at this time.' Rick did as ordered, showing no signs of embarrassment or arguing.

'Hmm,' Gran said unexpectedly. 'Nice pecs. Wouldn't you agree, Tammy?'

'Gran!'

I had to agree with her opinion — though it would have been inappropriate to show it.

'My dearest Tammy. Although I might be getting on a bit, I can still appreciate the physique of the male form. If I were forty years younger . . . '

'Mum. Stop making the youngsters uncomfortable,' said Amanda. Despite his obvious pain, Rick grinned.

Up until now Gran had been between me and Rick. She moved aside to gather some salves, and I shuddered.

Rick's body was a mess. Talk about literally being black and blue. I hadn't realised how badly he'd fallen until now.

'Can you fix him?' I asked my grandmother, my eyes becoming misty.

'He's not a broken toy, Tammy, but yes, I can 'fix' him. Amanda, would you please pass me that jar of Firestorm? Oh, and the Q-12 cream. While I do this, perhaps Tammy can pull herself together and explain what happened.'

I dried my eyes. Gran was right. Rick

was in good hands.

Quickly I found the files on Kyle and Lois, passing them first to Kim, who circulated them after a quick read. Meantime I related who Kyle had been to me and what had happened today at my apartment. Surprising myself, I was concise and factual, completing my report with my guess that this same grey powder had been used on me when I was twelve and missing for those two days.

'Since I woke up quickly, I believe that I had some sort of resistance to it — like when your immune system makes antibodies if you get chicken pox so you don't get them again. Rick came round once I'd vacuumed it all and put the canister in a sealed bin bag.'

Gran applied the last of the adhesive pads to Rick's battered body. Already he appeared to have recovered some-what and was now able to breathe normally.

'And that's the offending stuff in that rubbish bag? Good thinking, Tammy. I reckon you're reight and I reckon I ken what it is too. I'll need a guinea pig to test my theory, though. Someone who hasn't been exposed before. Obviously not Amanda. Perhaps you, Paul?'

Until now Paul had been very quiet. I imagined he was wondering what had happened to his sedate life. Even being married to a police Inspector wouldn't have prepared him for the turmoil he'd walked into. Amanda had told me he was a gentle, quiet guy who listened at parties rather than leading conversations.

'Yeah, I'll volunteer. It won't have any lasting effects on me, will it? Make me lose my hair or speak with a squeaky voice.'

We smiled. Paul was totally bald already, though he had an uncharacteristically tough, deep voice which belied his timid nature.

Gran took him and the rubbish bag to one side away from the rest of us. 'Best sit down, Paul,' she told him as she untied the bag and took a sniff herself. Then she bid him do the same. He collapsed right away, his head falling back against the cushioned seat.

Securing the bag again, she waited until Paul woke up, before turning to us.

'I know what this is and I'll dispose of it safely. Before you ask, I'll disinfect your vacuum cleaner bits too. It's one of my experimental concoctions that went missing years ago, a few months before you vanished for those two days, Tammy. I called it Dreamdust. Powerful stuff which knocks people out and takes their memory away of whatever goes on around them. I suspected whoever took you had used it, Tammy. I'm sorry.'

'But I woke up,' I pointed out.

'Like you suspected, your body builds up an immunity. It gradually wears off like a polio injection. Then you need a booster. You and Rick will be immune now, just like Kyle is. That's why it didn't make him unconscious.'

All this time, Kim had been multi-tasking, examining our files.

'DS Turpin told me you have a theory of where Lois's boat vanished to. Could I ask you to do some more detectiving, Tammy? DS Turpin is on sick leave as of now, so I'll assign another officer to accompany you. I need to get back to the rest of the team with this information. There are already officers up at the Manor House and digging into any connection between Lois and that funeral guy, Cyril Andover.'

I was eager to get going to test my theory about where the elusive Lois and her vanishing boat were hiding.

Rick was on the mend and I had a feeling that the situation with Lois, Kyle and the treasure was coming to a head. She'd done her sneaky searches on the quiet for over a decade, though now there was a major woman-hunt on and she was casting her anonymity to the wind. A day, maybe two, and I sensed they'd be gone, leaving us no chance of catching them.

Forty minutes later, Constable Steve MacDonald and I were down on the tow path by the canal. It was drizzling. I was wearing my tan anorak while Steve was in wet weather gear. He wasn't carrying a gun, but told me that instructions were to investigate only. If we discovered anything, he'd radio headquarters. The station wasn't far away.

Every now and then I'd check my photocopy of the library's ancient plans. They dated from just prior to 1800.

Steve was quite patient considering the less than clement weather. I tugged the hood over my face a bit. This needed careful, meticulous observation. We couldn't rush it. There had been two false alarms — branches marked for construction — though both had been closed and converted to other uses many years before.

We were alone apart from some stray

dog. Tourists weren't as keen to ramble along the picturesque pathway when the weather was like this. It was a Monday too.

Up ahead was another tunnel, this time cutting through a small hillside rather than simply going under a bridge.

'There's no towpath,' I observed as we drew closer.

'When they built it, the horse would have been taken around while the men on the boat lay on their backs and literally pushed the boat along by putting their feet on the low, curved roof of stones. It was called 'legging'.'

Steve had lived in the area his entire life.

'Why can't we see the light on the other side?'

'Must curve around before it comes out. We'll have to go over the top and rejoin the path on the other side,' he suggested.

'No. There's a narrow path at the side. You might have to duck. It'll be a

239

squeeze, but I want to be thorough.'

Steve wasn't keen, so I offered to go by myself, but he insisted we stay together. He poked his head in.

'It's too dark, Miss Jordan. Can't see a thing.'

I produced two flashlights.

'Come on, Constable. I've had my share of chickens today.'

Reluctantly he agreed, offering to go first. I took a long look around outside. The nearest structure was a derelict stone mill on the other side of the canal. Maybe, like my home, some enterprising developer would buy it and renovate it into high-end apartments for young couples and single professionals.

'Ready?' I called out. It would have to be single file and even I would need to watch my head. After the coal dust episode I wasn't keen to repeat the whole shampooing experience again tonight. Spiders, hundreds of years of soot and dirt . . . I should be getting danger money. Or at least a new bottle of VO5.

I played my flashlight around every few yards, stopping to do so. I didn't want to miss anything.

Steve, on the other hand, was in a hurry. I'd asked to slow down a few times yet he insisted there was nothing here and the pathway was slippery and dangerous from moss and lichen.

Just when I was inclined to agree with him, I slipped but managed to regain my balance just before I fell into the darkened waters at my side. My torch wasn't as lucky.

'You OK, Miss Jordan?' Big Mac asked from up in front.

'Yeah. I saw something over the other side. Shine your torch around.'

Steve turned his light onto the opposite wall. There was nothing but stone. Then I caught a glimpse of something not quite right.

'The ceiling. Shine it up there, please.'

Instead of the curved roof in this area, it was almost flat. Moreover, the flat part continued straight ahead

241

— whereas the tunnel continued to the right where the normal arched roof began once more.

'Shine it on the wall again, Constable. Where I'm pointing.' The wide beam of his torch showed my hand. 'There. Keep it steady.' I peered intently at the stonework. There was a vertical line and another identical one fifteen feet to the right. It didn't fit the normal brick-like staggered pattern of the stones all around.

'There's a false wall there. That's probably where Lois Griffiths and her boat are hiding. We must get out and call for assistance down here. You'll have to help me out into the light.'

Carefully we walked forward until we could see a semi-circle of light in the distance. Soon the pathway was lit up too. We emerged under a grove of birch trees that overhung the canal.

'Come on, Steve. Contact the police station. Kim . . . sorry DI Byrne should be there.'

I was excited. We were closing in on the villain.

'I'll try her mobile first. She asked to be told immediately.'

He lifted out his own mobile and dialled.

'It's message mode. DI Byrne? It's Constable MacDonald. We've found what appears to be a concealed tunnel on the canal. It's about two miles west of Hebden under a hill near . . . ' he looked up, 'The old Fitzwilliam Mill. Hurry up, pl . . . No. It cut off.'

'Try the station, please. It might be hours before she checks her messages.'

He did, finally speaking to a real person. After giving directions, he suggested a boat and armed officers.

They arrived in less than ten minutes, although the boat would take longer. Meanwhile I took Kim into the tunnel and pointed out the offending hidden door. Kim sent officers up to the mill with instructions to go down, as we believed there was access from there as well.

It seemed ages until the commandeered boat arrived. Although it had a powerful motor, there was a strict speed limit, even for the police.

Lights were brought in to illuminate the wall.

'Ma'am. There's a lever here,' one of the people on the boat shouted. Kim climbed on board while I stayed on the pathway.

Drawing her own weapon, Kim readied the three officers on the boat.

'Open it,' she ordered him.

The huge false wall slid laboriously to the side, revealing another water-filled passage. In the distance across the brightly lit cavern, we could all see the Mademoiselle A'Bor motoring away from us with a fading chug-chug-chug, disappearing into another darkened passageway.

'After her!' Kim said. The light craft surged through the hidden gap, only to lurch as metal screamed in torment. The boat was torn apart. I could see huge spikes just below the waterline.

The four crew members scrambled to safety as the boat sank into the black water.

I realised there were cries of pain. One of the officers had been injured; a huge red gash visible on his leg as he was helped onto the wide space in the tunnel where provisions were clearly stored.

The Mademoiselle disappeared triumphantly into the darkness.

Lois had eluded us once more.

12

Once upon a time, there was a despotic businessman with a plan. Lord Nibberton had been denied his preferred canal route through his land in the Valley where he could load his building stone directly onto barges — but that hadn't stopped his schemes to defile the countryside in his quest for money.

Once upon a time.

The trouble was, it now seemed there'd be no happy ending for this fairy tale.

His Nibs had built other feeder canals like the one I was now standing in. Lois had made her getaway at the leisurely speed of four miles an hour. If anyone could have pursued her on foot, she would have been caught almost immediately; however there was no sign of any tow path alongside the hidden tunnel.

The injured policeman had been taken to hospital in Halifax, though it seemed the wound from the jagged barrier was not serious.

'Tammy. Have a gander at this,' Kim called out. She was soaked from the sabotage of the boat, but apparently un-bothered.

I made my way across the wide expanse of floor by the side of the hidden canal.

It was evident Lois had been holing up here for a while, probably since I'd seen her on Saturday morning. It was well stocked with provisions, as well as a kitchen with a stove. There was also a closed-off area supplied with gas, hot water for a shower, plus a chemical toilet. She'd left her wigs and disguises, too.

'What am I supposed to see?' I asked. There were forensics gloves on my hands so I didn't contaminate the crime scene.

Kim indicated the three poorly-made beds in different parts of the area.

'Lois, Kyle and . . . ?' I wondered.

'Can only guess. Hopefully Darren Bruce. We can but hope,' the policewoman said.

I peered into the tunnel into which Lois had escaped.

'Any luck finding her?'

'Once we managed to disconnect her booby trap and get another boat here, we assumed we'd still catch her. No such luck. The tunnel only goes about half a mile then opens into a natural cavern; an underground lake. There are caves everywhere. She knows her way around in there. We don't. That's why we've given up the chase . . . for now. Still, we've found her hideout so she won't dare come back here.'

A small victory. Forensics were having another busy day of it.

'Ma'am. Over here,' a white-garbed figure with mask and white cap called out. I couldn't tell if it were a man or a woman in this echoey space.

I followed Kim and stared at the oxygen tanks and other scuba gear.

'Darren Bruce explores caves as a hobby. Probably he's a diver as well.'

Kim lifted a file and placed it in an evidence bag. 'We'll check that out. And here, some notes. I'll have a copy sent to you and your Scooby Doo gang.'

I grinned. Growing up, the American cartoon had been one of my favourite shows.

'You cheeky so and so, Kim Byrne. OK, who's who?'

'Amanda is the sensible one, Daphne; your gran is Velma and Rick is Shaggy.'

Thinking about it, Rick was a good Shaggy, the untidy, not-too-bright one with the messy hair. Then I realised, 'Hold on. Who am I?'

'Scooby Doo, obviously. Getting into trouble all the time — and you both have a cold, wet nose.'

Kim flicked some water onto the tip of my nose then walked off.

Ah well, Scooby and often Shaggy solved the mystery . . . usually by accident.

★ ★ ★

Back at Gran's place, I decided that another long shower was required before giving everyone the latest information on the elusive Lois and Kyle. Although Paul had originally been unhappy about Amanda's (and the baby's) involvement in this mad roller-coaster of danger, he was now eager to assist with collating information that was on all the documents we'd gathered.

More importantly he'd found the long-lost details that Darren had asked Gran about; family history from the time His Nibs had been around. I was certain that finding where the valuables were could be logically deduced by fitting all the clues together.

After my shower, Gran applied her miracle cure to the now very faint remnants of the Touch. She also gave me a lesson on understanding Homoeopathy and the medical benefits of plants. I was already a convert.

She told me Rick had rung earlier to

say he was much improved and was hoping to be back at work tomorrow.

We had an early dinner before settling down in Gran's lounge room to share the latest news.

Paul had tidied the room up, taking many of the boxes away to the tip and charity shops. This allowed us more space to fill with other boxes of our family's history.

Talk about a mess. But, with Paul's brilliant efforts, it was now an organised mess.

We all had our drinks of choice by our chairs. Wine for Paul and Gran; a bottle of fine Moselle which Paul had brought from his friend's winery in Bavaria. Amanda opted for a non-alcoholic beer as, surprisingly, did I. The excuse was that I wanted a clear head — though the truth was, I really didn't fancy alcohol any longer.

I decided that was a good thing. I'd seen what drink did to Mum and Dad and decided I wouldn't follow their lifestyle.

'We found old Eugene Hathaway's diaries. He was mayor of the area back when his Lordship Armageddon Nibberton was making a reight nuisance of hissen,' Gran began.

Wow! Armageddon as a first name. I could see why that had soon fallen out of fashion. Still, it did fit in with the extreme religious ideas and practices that existed back then.

Gran continued, preparing to read an excerpt from the still robust book. 'This seems to be particularly important for us today . . .

'*Although Armageddon Nibberton does profess to be a gentleman of high and exalted standing within our fine community, he thinks nowt of inflicting cruel and barbaric torment upon the bodies and souls of those poor wretches, men, women and children who are in his employ.*

'*I myself have oft had occasion to object most strenuously to his conduct and demeanour, only to be threatened by his collective of Scuttlers from*

Manchester. I was fortunate not to receive a most complete drubbing at their hands.

'Post Scriptum: It is indeed felicitous that he knows not of the sanctum where lies the Thesaurum for, if he were to perceive its cache, he would surely claim it as his own, contrary to the promise to bestow it upon the masses.

The spectres of the Dark Waters have kept their silent counsel long enough. I pray that they continue to do so.'

'There's a few terms I don't know, Gran. 'Thesaurum' and 'Scuttlers'.'

'That's a surprise. I thought you knew everything.' Amanda gave me a cheeky wink. I poked out my tongue.

'Don't fret, Tammy,' Paul responded with a smile at our family fun. 'We had to look them up, in a dictionary and that huge encyclopaedia some fast-talking salesman convinced your grandmother to buy. 'Thesaurum' is a treasure hoard and the 'Scuttlers' were gangs of thugs around two hundred years ago.'

'Therefore, we have more clues. 'Dark waters' probably refers to that underground lake we found today. It's not on any maps.'

Gran was surprised. 'You're telling us that it does exist? I'd heard rumours over the years — water-filled caverns in the limestone pockets down below the sandstone.'

'I saw them with my own eyes,' I said. 'Lois escaped through them. By the way, there are more signs that the mis-per, Darren, might be still alive.'

That brought a tear to Amanda's eye. I recalled that she'd been closely involved with the case before her maternity leave.

Eventually I took my leave to use Amanda's computer to catch up on work. Adventuring was one thing. However, I did still need to pay the bills.

'Before I say goodnight, could I borrow that diary of our ancestors? There might be something else he says about the medieval fortune.'

They agreed. Before going upstairs, I thought I'd give Rick a call on my mobile. I went outside to view the spectacular multi-hued sunset.

Talking to him, while the sky bid farewell to another day, was perfect. I wondered what escapades tomorrow would bring.

★ ★ ★

Sleep was supposed to be a way for, not only the body to recharge, but also the brain. Our minds must be like a library with books being taken from the shelves to be read throughout the day. Every evening the librarians return them to the right place.

My own mind must have been trying to make sense out of the complex questions from the past few days because now, as I woke up, all I could think of was some glaring thing that simply made no sense about the Manor.

At breakfast, I told everyone what

was bothering me. They agreed.

'Rick and I are returning to have another detailed investigation of the basement. He's feeling more like his old self, Gran. He was amazed the damage healed so quickly.'

She gave me one of her cheeky winks from behind her glasses.

'Believe me, the pleasure was all mine. He's a fine young man.'

Rick arrived at ten-ish. Before I could join him with our bag full of exploring goodies, another police car pulled up next to us. It was Constable Mac-Donald in uniform.

'DI Byrne asked me to tag along, DS Turpin. Said after what happened yesterday, you needed back-up.'

'Yes, I know, Constable. Even so, I thought there were two other officers assigned to come.'

Big Mac donned some work overalls and boots, similar to those Rick was wearing.

'Last-minute plan change. I assumed they'd told you. I'm more familiar with the case — and this neck of the woods.'

I sensed Rick wasn't very happy about this. Whether it was their history or whether it was not being consulted about the change, I didn't know. Since we were all travelling up to the Manor together, we couldn't really discuss the reason for his unease.

I sat in the back seat by choice. As we drove up Arcana Valley, it gave me a chance to peruse the original plans for the Manor House. Clearly not everything that was actually there appeared on the blueprints.

The position of the property intrigued me. It would have been more sensible to build the structure at the top of the hill, where it was flat. He owned the entire hill. Why, given his well-documented megalomania, would he choose to build on the slope? It would certainly have been more costly.

'Where to first, Tammy?' Rick asked as we carried our tools and such inside. Technically there was no private owner now. Lois Griffiths had forfeited that right through her continual non-payment of outstanding bills to the council. It was a moot legal point, but the property was derelict and was not locked when the police had first visited on Saturday.

'Basement. Think about it, Rick. There was a secret door to the basement — one that had been used quite a lot recently. It had a generator but nothing else that was of interest.'

'You forgot the coal,' said Rick with a sly grin.

'I'll never, ever forget that horrible black stuff,' I replied, nudging him. He moaned a little. Oh, crumbs. The bruising from yesterday. I apologised immediately.

We went to the kitchen, where I deftly opened the hidden entrance to the underground room.

'We need to make sure it stays open. There's the mechanism. Disable the closing bits or the timer. If you can't do that, prop it open with the kitchen table. We do not want to be trapped down there again.'

Rick found the timing device; a clockwork mechanism. He disconnected it from the closer. I decided he must be well used to tinkering with ancient machines, having had practice with his rust-bucket VW Beetle.

We descended the stone steps with some more fuel for the generator. After topping it up, Big Mac started it and the flickering lights illuminated the room. Bit by bit, I examined the walls and floor for any signs of a concealed door or hiding place. The others did the same.

There had to be something here. After all, His Nibs installed the top door for a reason. He must have.

'There's absolutely nothing, Tammy. We've looked everywhere,' Rick admitted, conceding defeat after fruitless minutes of poking around.

'I have to agree, Miss Jordan.'

'OK. We'll leave the generator on so there's power upstairs. I still believe there's something important and it's there to be found.'

We headed back up the stairs against the wall, me at the rear. I touched the stones for support then, on impulse, put my hand on the stairs, feeling around on the joint.

Through a tiny gap I could feel fresh air blowing upwards. Why? Suddenly, I had a thought.

'Hold on, guys. Come on back down. There's one place we haven't checked.'

Returning to the basement, Rick glanced around, intrigued. I shone the light on the wall the stairs were against.

'There.' Excitedly, I pointed to a loose stone jutting out, slightly proud of the other sandstone blocks.

Rick reached to touch it. Nothing happened. He pushed it, right and then left. Still nothing.

'Try the top,' I suggested, crossing my fingers. The false stone rotated. Immediately unseen gears began turning behind the seemingly solid structure and the base of the stairs inched outwards, hinged by the wall under the kitchen entrance.

'Well, I'll be . . . ' Rick muttered. 'You were right, Tammy. Another hidden entrance.'

The entire staircase swung wider, revealing a passageway. It was illuminated by the same flickering lamps in the basement. They must have been connected to the generator too.

A gentle, damp, cold breeze enveloped us.

'Any idea where that passageway leads?' Steve asked.

'At a guess, I believe it will go down and meet up with the same underground lake or river that we found yesterday, Constable.'

Dark Waters, my ancestor called it. Was the hoard of valuables down there too — or had Lois and Kyle already found them?

★　★　★

The tunnel was wide and, although electric bulbs were strung along the walls, the passageway felt ominous. Steve suggested a precaution that made a lot of sense.

'I'll go outside and call it in. The station needs to be aware of what you've discovered. I'll ask for back-up too.'

'And tell them how to open it if it swings shut again. We'll try to brace it open,' I suggested, deciding to take my own precautions to ensure the back-up team wouldn't miss the entrance if it did close.

After Steve left, I searched my pockets for my favourite lipstick, showing it to Rick.

'A girl's best friend. First a touch-up for my lips, then there . . . ' I said, pointing.

Rick nodded. 'Good idea, precious.'

Steve returned from outside within minutes.

'They're on their way. Shouldn't be long. Shall we wait or . . . ?'

I decided not to. 'Let's go. They'll catch us up. There's already two of you, so we should be safe. Besides, I'm eager to see if we can find this Darren guy.'

Rick turned to me in the eerie half light of the oppressive basement.

'Tammy. What is it with you? You don't need to be doing this. In fact, you shouldn't be here. You're not police. It's our job, not yours.'

There was real concern in his voice.

'I've been wondering about that myself. In a way, I feel responsible even though I'm not. In the past few days, a new part of me has emerged. The old me would be standing back, watching others do the dangerous things — but I'm not that timid woman any longer.

'Lois and Kyle have been screwing up my life for too long; not only for me, either. I need to be involved and I really want to help. I discovered this hidden tunnel, didn't I?'

Rick touched my cheek tenderly.

'I don't want to put you in danger, Tammy.'

'You're not. Come on. And watch your step. It seems the rain from last week has been seeping through. The ground seems quite soggy.'

Gingerly we set off down the sloping path. The tunnel was well supported where it needed to be. This was the reason His Nibs built the Manor House on the slope rather than the top. Less of a distance to tunnel to the limestone caverns he'd somehow discovered, which riddled the ground like holes in Swiss cheese.

From behind us, we heard the heavy door close despite the precautions we'd taken. No problem. I'd found a release switch on our side.

The electric lighting became sparser so we used our flashlights to navigate through the twisting caves. The surface underfoot was fairly level, with only the odd stalagmite indicating that the cave was fighting back against His Lordship's efforts to level the passage as much as possible. I suspected he'd taken horses and carts down the immense tunnels, from long abandoned passageways that we passed.

'Everyone stop for a sec. Turn off the torches.' I said, sensing a gradual change in our pathway over the past few hundred feet. The cables of electric lights had long since stopped. Also, the remnants of oil-fuelled torches fixed to the walls had gone. There was only one explanation.

The air was dank with mossy humidity and my voice echoed between the walls as we switched off our only lights one by one. I held my own breath although I could hear Rick and Big Mac breathing steadily.

'What . . . what's that?' Steve asked.

'Don't turn any lights on. Our eyes will adjust,' I told them. 'It's bioluminescence; some living things emitting their own light.'

Gradually the entire area around us assumed a bluish glow made up of thousands — no, millions — of tiny lights. It was a chemical reaction.

'Like fireflies? Glow worms?' Rick said.

'Exactly. Some bacteria and fungi do

it too. Considering where we are, I doubt any self-respecting insect would be this far down.'

We all could now see well enough to walk without use of artificial light. It was unnatural, but this set of caves was just that. It wasn't one of those horror-movie sensations where the hairs on the back of your neck stood erect, though there certainly was an overwhelming aura of history. Roman legionaries, medieval knights, brow-beaten labourers employed by His Lordship, all could have tramped through here. Their souls seemed to infuse the very atmosphere about us with phantom whispers, just like those I'd heard near the plague memorial at Sherwood.

Eventually, the pathway levelled and opened out onto a vast subterranean lake. Even the water glowed as it lapped gently at our feet. It seemed that movement stimulated the bioluminescence.

'Wow,' I exclaimed. 'Big, big super-wow.'

It almost took my breath away. The

azure blueness pulsed and sparkled in waves of radiance all about us like fairy lights on a Christmas tree.

I was so entranced by the spectacle, it took a nudge from Rick to remind me why we were in this place.

'Over there. On the next cove.'

He was right. There were a number of shacks arranged along the shoreline, along with a jetty. Another hiding place for Lois and company.

'Doesn't look as if anyone's at home,' Steve observed. 'No boat, and no movement. Shall we?'

It was obvious that we should. Perhaps Darren might be there, locked up somehow. I assumed he'd been taken weeks before due to his diving skills. Lois must have thought she had been close to unearthing the riches she thought had been secreted, to have taken such a brazen risk.

We approached the cluster of wooden huts cautiously only to find they were indeed uninhabited — though, like the canalside cavern, they'd been used recently. Inside we turned on our torches.

★ ★ ★

In retrospect we should have posted a look-out. The various maps of this underground maze had me so engrossed, I didn't hear our enemies approaching until it was too late.

'It's polite to knock before entering someone's property, Miss Jordan — and friends.'

Spinning around, we were confronted by a red-haired woman and Kyle, who was wielding a knife.

'Lois Griffiths, I presume?' I answered this shrill-voiced woman who had been the curse of my life.

'I prefer Lady Nibberton,' was her scornful response. I was quite certain she had no claim to this title; His Nibs had been stripped of it after being jailed for stealing in his latter days of destitution.

Kyle made a move towards me but

Rick shifted forward too, brandishing a formidable chunk of wood he'd lifted from a makeshift work bench.

'Time for some answers, lady — '

It was only then I noticed a thin man standing in the background. He seemed so feeble he might collapse at any time. It must have been Darren Bruce. His eyes were blank and unfocused. Dear Lord, what had they done to him?

'A Nibberton does not reply to the likes of you, Miss Jordan. Your family always believed they were better than mine, especially your grandfather with his pretentious do-gooder attitude. We Nibbertons were chosen to rule this part of the countryside. And once one has one's rightful inheritance, we will hound you out of Arcana Valley and all of Calderdale.'

Her green eyes flared with anger. She was clearly in possession of her ancestors' despotic genes as well as delusions of grandeur.

Kyle started to say something causing Lois to fling her gaze around to him, her neatly braided hair flying around like a horse's tail at dressage. Her pink dress and coat were soiled and torn. Yet it was that seething fury permeating her features which was the saddest aspect of my nemesis.

'Shut your mouth, Kyle. You always did have a soft spot for her, ever since we took her and infected her with The Touch. You should have left her be — but no, you had to make a pest of yourself, following her. You deserve better than this know-it-all tramp. Once we get our monies, you'll have your share of beautiful girls flocking after you . . . film stars, heiresses, royalty, even that Britney bimbo singer you always listen to. I only gave you this Jordan woman's latest address so you could bring her here, though you even mucked that up. You're useless, Kyle — just like your no-hoper father, wherever he is.'

Interesting. Mother and son, bickering. Time to stir things up a bit.

'Lovely to see you again, Mr

270

Chicken. What was it you told me, Rick? Oh yeah, you said he almost wet his pants, he was so scared.'

Kyle took the bait. He almost lost it then. He certainly had a short temper, just like his mother.

'Care to tell me what this is all about, Kyle? Or do you have to ask Mummy first?'

Kyle bristled again but Lois realised what I was trying to do. She took a step back and sat down in a chair, massaging her hands. I suspected she had problems from being down here in this dank, cool place so much. She was only in her fifties though she appeared far older.

'No need, Kyle. I'll tell Miss Clever Clogs. When we moved into the Manor years ago, we had no idea there were riches down here. I was working with that crazy Cyril as a part-time assistant while I was at the Post Office. He wasn't all there, but most of his clients just thought him eccentric.

'He let it drop one day after he'd had

too much to drink. That's when he told me the story about the treasure.'

Lois paused to wipe her mouth.

'Then it was a case of checking records and searching the Manor House until we found the tunnels. It was our inheritance, but your family would have stopped us. Cyril told us all about you self-proclaimed Guardians of the Valley.' Her tone became, if possible, even more vindictive.

'You might not think it to look at me, but I'm a good 'un for planning ahead. I thought since your grandparents and me were going to be adversaries, I needed to distract them — put 'em off my scent, so to speak.

'That's when I captured you, gave you some of that Dreamdust I got your mother to steal from your gran, then set your mum and gran at one another's throats. Your mother . . . well, she liked her drink. It was easy to poison her mind.

'She took you away from your grandparents, a sickly young girl infected with The Touch. It broke your grandparents' hearts 'cause they doted on you. Their aim was to make you a Guardian like them. I made sure that never happened.'

I nodded. 'Intercepting our mail certainly kept us apart, Lois. I detest you for that.'

'Don't care, you little brat. I might not be clever like you but I knew that in time I could find the Nibberton fortune. Took us years to find the passage under the Manor and this lake.'

I couldn't resist a smirk.

'Took me, er . . . let's see . . . five days?'

Lois sneered, baring her teeth.

'Like I said, too clever by half.'

'Why not kill me when I was young?' I asked.

'We're not murderers. Besides, what we did to you was much worse for you and those stuck-up grandparents of yours.'

That was a relief. I imagined her

threats to us were empty ones. Even Robin Hood had been pretending with his bow and arrow, as he said.

Rick and Kyle still had weapons, but had dropped their arms down due to the weight of them.

Darren had been kidnapped; that meant prison for Lois and Kyle. Hopefully the doctors could sort Darren out. At present he seemed to be in a daze, just like a zombie; some variant of that Dreamdust perhaps.

'Better give yourself up now, you two.' I could get other answers later.

'And why should we do that, Miss Clever Clogs?' Lois was on her feet again, surprisingly belligerent.

'Simple maths. There's two of you and three of us. Besides, more police should be here any moment.'

I took a quick look around. Where was Steve? Suddenly he appeared from behind me, pushing me to the dirt floor and disarming Rick before he could fight back.

We'd been betrayed. Big Mac was

working for Lois. As for our reinforcements, I doubted they'd ever been called.

Lois stood over me, a hypodermic in her hand.

'What were you saying about maths, Miss Clever Clogs?' Then she plunged the needle into my arm.

13

I watched the drama unfold as wooziness overtook my senses. It was not as immediate or as strong as that Dreamdust Kyle had used on us yesterday.

Though a haze and unable to move, I watched as both Steve and Kyle held Rick while Lois injected him too.

We were in real trouble now, and there was no hope of rescue thanks to the deceit of Big Mac. In a flash, I understood that he must have been the officer Gran had spoken to about Darren all those weeks ago. No wonder she'd never been interviewed.

'Now what?' the crooked copper asked as Rick also slumped into submission.

'I might hate her family so much, but she is one clever cow. She tracked us down and now we've nowhere to run.

Did she mention anything to the other police?' Lois was concerned.

'Only that we were coming to the Manor House. The basement stairs have closed, leaving no trace of where the entrance is. My thicko colleagues will never work out the opening, so we're safe for the moment.'

Lois paused as though weighing up her options.

'I wonder. Maybe Miss Clever Clogs has worked out where the treasure is as well.'

'I doubt it,' Kyle said, glaring down at me. 'I've been trying to find it for years. And I'm no dummy.'

'Kyle. You're twenty-five and still can't tie your shoelaces. Of course, you're a dummy, but you're my son and I love you anyway. That injection saps a person's free will. She'll have to tell the truth if I ask her. I'm thinking now that I did the wrong thing, keeping her away from here all them years. Still, no use wanting to change the past.'

She stared at me in the yellow

semi-glow of the lights. 'Tammy. Stand up.'

I didn't move. She took a deep breath and, in a commanding, albeit slightly croaky voice, told me,

'Stand. Stand up, I say.'

I pushed myself to my feet, staring blankly at her.

'Do you have any idea where the Catholic jewels and precious metals have been buried?'

In muted tones, I replied, 'Yes. I think so.'

'Well, I'm waiting, you stupid woman. Where are they?'

'The Spectres of the Dark Waters. It's where my ancestor, Eugene Hathaway, said they were in his diary,' I said in a monotone.

'Spectres? What the blazes does that mean?' Lois yelled, obviously exasperated. I kept silent.

'It's another word for ghosts, Mum. Like the ones near the memorial.'

Big Mac seemed lost. 'Memorial?'

'Rooster, my darling young man. You

just might be right.' Lois kissed him on both cheeks, much to his annoyance. 'Come on. Everyone, get onto the boat. We're going on a short trip. And, Steve, the memorial is a tribute to our ancestor, Lord Nibberton the first. There's a shrine we built to him on the other side of the lake. There are three limestone pillars there that look like ghosts against the blackened walls.'

We were all told to walk, with Lois and her two henchmen, Kyle and Big Mac. Darren and Rick were like robots doing as Lois told them. I pretended to be in the same drug-induced stupor. Actually, whatever was in that syringe had worn off me in seconds, possibly due to my exposure to Dreamdust all of those years before — plus Kyle's tossing it over us yesterday.

I'd realised immediately that I would be no match for the three of them at this time. But at some point I could escape — hopefully not before trapping them first.

'Tammy. Walk up the gangplank onto

my boat. Sit at the bow.'

I did as Lois ordered. Rick was seated by my side. The blue glow all around was bright enough to see clearly. I still found it hard to comprehend that this magical fairy land could exist down here in the bowels of the earth.

It was imperative that I didn't endanger my fellow prisoners, I reminded myself.

We cast off and were soon motoring along. Behind us the churned-up water from the propellers gleamed brighter, turning almost white in the boat's wake. It was exquisite.

Strangely, I noticed another blue wake behind up and to one side. A shadowy silhouette kept pace with us before diving under the surface and vanishing. The others didn't mention it, even though the creature must have been thirty feet in length.

Kyle was at the stern of the wooden craft, holding the wheel. Lois cupped her hands around her mouth and called out. 'Steer to port, Kyle . . . not the right, you pillock. The left. Port is left, starboard is right. How many times?'

She sat down opposite Darren, Rick and me before turning to Steve.

'I despair about that boy, I really do. The trouble with the Nibberton family in Arcana Valley was inbreeding. I'm afraid my son is the result of too many bad genes getting together. Trouble was, he became infatuated with that Tammy girl when we kidnapped her. Never got over her. Even renamed his favourite teddy bear after her.'

I think Big Mac was becoming bored with talk of Kyle. It was obvious he disliked Lois's son.

He asked her some details about the memorial then added, 'I might have some suggestions where the treasure is. After all, you promised me ten per cent of it for keeping the cops away.'

Lois responded, 'We found some remains down here a few years back. There was a ring that had fallen off his hand. The inscription read *Armageddon Nibberton.*'

'Must have been a dammed big ring,' Big Mac muttered. Lois gave no sign of hearing his sarcastic observation.

'Got it cleaned up and now it hangs around my neck, just to remind me that I'm royalty. See?' She pulled it from inside her blouse to show Rick. He gave it a cursory glance.

'You reckon it's his Lordship and he must have died out here?'

Lois continued. 'I know they never found his body. I guess he died searching for the fortune. He dedicated his life to it, just like Kyle and me.'

Steve stood up to peer at the far wall of the cavern that we were approaching.

'Is that it over there, with some candles? What are those white columns on the right? Are they the ghosts?'

'We reckon. There's nothing like them anywhere else. Kyle and me explored it all over the years after we found the secret entrance near Hebden. The tunnels go everywhere.'

Steve continued. 'One thing I could never suss out, Lois. If his Lordship discovered all of this why didn't he use the lake and tunnels to move stone from Arcana Valley through to the Rochdale Canal? It would have been cheaper and faster.'

'He tried, Steve. He really tried. Trouble was, there were no tow paths for horses and, without a motor like on the Mademoiselle here, the only other way was to use men to row all the way. It was too hard and too far. Finding that treasure would have been his salvation.'

'How did he know it was around here, Lois? I can't imagine the Catholic Church wanted it to be common knowledge when Henry was taking everything they once owned for himself or the Church of England?'

'There was an old monastery that had been sacked during the Reformation. Someone found some papers in Latin buried under the ruins and gave them to my ancestor.'

We were slowing down now. The shrine to Lord Nibberton was clearly visible. In the middle were the remains of a person — His Lordship presumably. Flashlights played over the corpse. I almost gasped at the sight, having been expecting a pile of bones.

Instead, it seemed that this mysterious place somehow kept things from decaying. Sunken eyes stared back at me from sullen features on a man who had died in great pain or from shock. I felt sorry for him, alone and forever preserved for over one hundred fifty years.

Steve tried to hide a shudder.

'Poor old man. He seems to be staring towards your ghost rocks — even reaching out to them.'

Lois peered at her dead ancestor.

'You're absolutely right, Steve. Funny . . . I never noticed that before.'

The boat was stopping. I assumed that navigating any closer would be dangerous due to rocks below. Lois faced her son again at the other end of the long, narrow vessel.

'Oi, Kyle. Drop the anchor and get the dinghy ready.' The cavern echoed with the sound of her dreadful voice. She lowered her volume. 'Steve. You stay here and keep watch over these three. They won't do a thing unless you tell them, so they won't be any trouble.'

Lois was clambering along the side of the lengthy cabin when she realised something.

'We need more petrol for the dinghy motor. You, Tammy. You get the container from the galley under the sink. It's in a red plastic jerry can. Take it to us at the stern. Do you understand?'

'Yes. I understand,' I replied slowly in my best monotone before clambering down into the long cabin. If Lois and Kyle were leaving the boat, then I needed to keep them from returning. What better way than to incapacitate their dinghy?

Years ago, I'd read that sugar in petrol would destroy an engine as it would gum up the works. That seemed like an urban myth. Sugar wouldn't dissolve and would just sink to the bottom.

I decided water was a better bet. It would sink to the bottom of the jerry can but when tipped up, the water would be likely to end up in the fuel tank on the small boat. I didn't want to disable the engine immediately.

It only took a minute to add a bottle of water before I took the container to Lois and Kyle. Once there I stood impassively as I watched them step into the dinghy and add the mixture.

'You. Tammy. Go back the front of the boat and sit down,' Lois ordered me as they readied the tiny boat.

I returned through the kitchen, desperately wondering what to use to subdue Big Mac once the others were well away from the boat. A frying pan? A kitchen knife? Realistically, they were out of the question. I wasn't a fighter and Steve was far stronger than me. Before I could decide on anything,

Steve appeared at the top of the steps to the bow.

'Here. What's taking you so long?'

I couldn't let him be suspicious.

'I fell over,' I replied in my best zombie voice. He eyed me suspiciously as I made my way past him, up the steps and sat down next to Rick just as the Lois and Kyle expedition passed the bow of the boat.

Rats. I hadn't managed to snatch anything from the galley. Now I was defenceless. There was nothing around on the wooden deck or seats that I could use.

By now Lois and Kyle were chuffing along to the narrow beach between His Nibs's body and the three spectral figures made of rock. The motor began to miss occasionally as they hit the beach. I assume water was getting into the pistons or whatever made the motor work.

Rick and Darren were staring blankly straight ahead into the blue-twinkling blackness of the cavern. Fortunately, I was sitting so that I could watch my would-be captors in their quest for the riches long since concealed down here. Lois was scrambling up the fallen rubble towards the phantom figures.

Steve was shining a large torch in their direction. There was a glint of light reflected from some shiny object near the feet of the first spectre.

'Lois. I saw . . . ' Steve shouted.

'I saw it too. Just down here.'

She knelt down carefully to examine the area.

'Watch yourself, Mum. Let me.' Kyle climbed up quickly to be beside her.

He scrambled around, suddenly shouting for joy as he lifted the glistening jewel high above his head.

'We've found it. We're rich. We're flaming rich!' he screamed almost deafening us all with the reverberations of his words. Kyle was ecstatic, almost slipping down from his precarious perch.

Even Steve had all his attention on them. I should have acted but I was intrigued. What if I'd done the wrong thing by repeating Eugene Hathaway's clue to its location? Had I guessed wrong?

'It's one precious stone, Kyle. Where's the rest? There should literally be hundreds of pieces of jewellery and expensive metals. Diamonds, emeralds, rubies . . . Wait. What's that opening?'

She pointed. Kyle grasped some hitherto unseen handle and pulled a huge concealed plate of metal to one side, sending it tumbling into the water with a fluorescent blue splash.

I held my breath, standing in my haste to get a better view. I didn't have long to wait.

Torches flashed around, searching the cache. I finally had my answer — as did the villains.

'It's gone. It's all gone. SOMEONE'S STOLEN MY INHERITANCE!' Lois howled before throwing her flashlight at the stone wall.

★   ★   ★

Steve swiftly turned his head, catching sight of my face in the blue light.

'What are you smiling at?' he began before making eye contact with me. It was no use pretending any longer.

'You. You're not in a trance at all.' He tried to move his whole body around so he could confront me head-on, but I had other plans.

I threw my weight against the side of the boat, causing it to rock from side to side. It wasn't enough . . . just sufficient to upset Steve's precarious balance.

He lurched from one side to the other before regaining his footing, then closing in on me. I staggered to the cabin steps just in time to avoid his grasping hands but, in this confined deck space, my time was running out.

Worse still, Rick and Darren hadn't moved. Talk about there never being a man around when you needed him. Except in this case, Rick was right here. Yet he may as well as been miles away for all the use he was.

'Say your prayers, girlie,' Steve

snarled, taking another step closer.

'Rick. Save me!' I yelled in desperation before Steve blocked my view of my friend.

This was surely it. The end . . .

14

It was a desperate plea. To my amazement, Rick stood and hit Steve from behind — though it was a very weak blow.

I needed to be specific. The element of surprise would only last so long.

Steve shrugged off Rick's pathetic attack and was turning to defend himself by striking back.

'Rick. Hit Steve hard.'

My young zombie here would be no match for Big Mac simply because he couldn't think for himself. It was up to me to save us both.

I waited until Steve was slightly off balance then rammed into him with every bit of strength I had. It was like hitting a brick wall, but it made him start whirling his arms to regain his footing.

'Rick. Push him overboard.'

We both hit Steve on the same side. He teetered once . . . twice . . . then plunged over the edge of the bow seating with a desperate cry. The splash soaked us all.

'Help! I can't swim.' Steve was flailing around in the dark waters surrounded by a blue halo from the agitated bacteria.

Looking around, I spied a life-saving ring which I hurled into the water over Steve's head.

He could probably have stood up. In any case, I didn't want him clambering back on board.

As Steve floundered in an awkward dog-paddle towards the float, I became aware of Lois voicing a string of shrill obscenities.

'Get the motor going, you blithering idiot, Kyle. If they sail off, we'll be stranded here.' She stood up to shake her fists at me. 'You absolute cow, Tamara. When I get my hands on you, I'll . . .'

More vindictive words followed. I

ignored them, even the very personal ones. They were stranded there on the beach. Kyle was trying to pull the starter cord on the outboard motor, but all that happened were splutters of a dead engine. The water in the petrol tank had worked.

Rick was standing stationary again, like a mannequin in a store window. Apart from the occasional blink, he was sadly lacking in any animation.

'No time for complacency, DS Turpin. Follow me.' I needed to start the canal boat engine and sail out of here. Meanwhile Big Mac had managed to grasp the life-saver and was splashing his way slowly to the shore. I didn't want to be here if they managed to fix the dinghy engine.

Once down at the stern, we managed to start up the motor and raise the anchor.

'Do you know how to drive this thing, Rick?'

'No,' was his monosyllabic response.

I took the wheel and throttle myself.

How hard could it be?

Harder than it looked, I found out before getting the hang of it. Which way to head?

Gazing around at the bleak blackness of the water, I decide that following those patches that were blue from agitation, especially the jagged, lighter blue pathway, was the way to go. Presumably that had been the way we came. It was like a trail of breadcrumbs laid by Hansel and Gretel.

Lois's wailings sounded like some demented banshee. If I didn't know the cause, it would be quite disconcerting in the darkness.

I was elated at trapping the three of them there. Once back on shore, all we needed to do was traipse the mile or so up the steep winding passageway to the Manor House, call for reinforcements then relax with a packet of custard creams . . . or maybe two.

The villain and her cohorts had been bested by little old me with a smidgen of help from Rick. Simple. I decided a celebratory kiss was in order.

'Rick. Come over here and bend down so I can reach you. Pucker your lips and close your eyes.'

I stood on my tiptoes and gave him the most passionate kiss I could.

Sadly, it was like touching lips with a one of those fish on ice in the supermarket.

'Rick. That was pathetic. Absolutely pa . . . thet . . . ic. I sincerely trust you can give a better account of yourself once that paralysing drug has worn off. Otherwise there will be no chance of me becoming Mrs Tammy Turpin.'

Not that there ever would be. The thought of being called that name was scarier than Lois in one of her rages. Perhaps this would be one of those modern marriages where I'd keep my maiden name.

'I love you anyway, Mr Rick Turpin,' I told him as he reverted to his mannequin stance.

★ ★ ★

It took only a few minutes of sailing across the sea of shadows before we could see movement near Lois's hideaway.

'Surely they can't have escaped! No — there's more than three of them.'

It was at that moment I heard Kim calling out.

'Tammy. Is that you?'

Admittedly it was difficult to hear her over the echoes of Lois's lament from far behind us. Good Lord — that woman had quite a voice on her.

'Yes, it's us. All safe and sound. There is one thing, though — I've no idea how to stop this thing by the jetty. And I really don't want to ram you or run aground.'

Kim replied, 'Just come to a stop out there. We've found a rowing boat. Some of my officers will come out, then bring the boat in safely.'

'Just so long as they're not homicidal maniacs like Big Mac, please. He and I have had . . . well, a falling out, big time.'

I watched as they set off towards us. It took only a few minutes before we alighted onto the jetty where Kim and four other officers were waiting. It was clear they were all amazed at this underground fairy grotto, looking around in wonder.

'Careful with the guys. They've been zombified by some injection. Rick did help me beat the crims — even though he probably won't remember it. The other man is Darren Bruce.'

'Well done, Tammy. We'll send the men to hospital for treatment. So where are Lois and company?'

I pointed across the water.

'I left them stranded on a beach near the remains of old man Nibberton. Lois and the Take-Away Twins.'

Kim seemed puzzled so I elaborated.

'Big Mac, also known as Steve MacDonald, and KFC, aka Kyle Francis Costello.'

That brought a smile to her face in the eerie combination of dim electric light and the blue glow.

'And that dreadful sound?' Kim asked.

'Lois. She's a trifle upset. Someone nicked her valuables.'

'Who did? Was it you?' Kim seemed intrigued.

'No . . . but I know who did.'

Kim made arrangements to care for my two stupefied companions, then we set sail back through the tunnels on the good ship Mademoiselle A'Bor with some armed officers on board. I navigated, while someone else piloted the boat . . . someone who was actually competent in what they were doing.

I had to ask Kim a question that had been bothering me.

'Why did you come searching for us so quickly?'

'Ah. Now that's a story in itself, young Tammy. Constable Steve Mac-Donald pushed his luck too far. Today he changed places with the two officers whom I'd assigned to come with you and DS Turpin. He told them it was my decision. One of them checked with me. It was then we realised he was keeping a close eye on you for Lois.'

'Like yesterday down at the Rochdale Canal end. Not only did he try to talk me out of exploring the tunnel, I bet he phoned Lois, pretending to be leaving a message on your phone. That's how she knew we were about to burst in on her little hiding place and made her getaway.'

I thought about when I'd first met the devious Steve. 'And it now seems that his saving me from Robin Hood was a set-up to get my confidence. Yours, too.'

Kim agreed. 'I must admit it was clever of you to mark the basement stone with pink lipstick. Otherwise we'd never have found the way into the tunnel.'

'Thinking ahead. Plus, maybe a part of me distrusted Steve. I will need some new lippy, though.'

Lois's dulcet tones were closer now. She could see the boat approaching in the darkness and she decided to step up the volume.

'Come back for us, eh, you horrible Hathaway hussy? Guilty conscience — or did you get yourself lost?'

I called back to her.

'I actually brought some of my friends, Lois, and they have handcuffs. You can come peacefully or we can leave you with your less than healthy ancestor for another day or two?'

Kyle began yelling. 'Well, you can all get lost. Go on — leave us for a few days — we don't care. Tell ya what? You can even leave us for a month. So there.'

We heard a crack and Kyle screaming in pain.

'Please ignore my less than brilliant son. He'll be the first to complain if he doesn't get his tea on time. We surrender.'

Her voice said it all. She was beaten and had no where to go.

'What about you, ex-Constable Mac-Donald?' Kim shouted. 'Do you give up too?'

'Yes, DI Byrne. No treasure means

no money for me, anyway. I'm truly sorry for betraying you all.' Steve sounded contrite.

Approaching their location, large lights were switched on to illuminate the macabre scene. Kim and the young policewoman by my side swore. One of the male officers crossed himself as though to ward off demons.

The three plotters were seated on the beach, shielding their eyes from the intense glare. To the right, the three spectral figures stood impassively guarding a now vanished hoard of precious gems and metals. Lastly there was His Nibs; death never looked so terrifying.

Another officer was filming the whole sorry episode. It would be one of those scenes we'd be haunted by for the rest of our lives.

* * *

Once retrieved in the other dinghy, all three miscreants were seated on the floor of the Mademoiselle, hands cuffed behind their backs. We were heading back to the jetty.

'What did you do to me all those years ago, Lois?' I asked.

She looked up at me, that sneer still on her face. She'd never forgive me but I sensed that someday soon, I'd find it in my heart to forgive her.

She wasn't pure evil as I thought . . . simply as twisted as those gnarled trees around Nibberton Manor. Possibly whatever had damaged them had affected her mind as well.

'I planned to snatch you when you were twelve; when you were the apple of your grandparents' eyes. We hid you here, drugged you up and let you go near the tunnel near Hebden. We were counting on you catching the Touch. It's more likely around those blue lights. Once you had it, we let you go.'

That explained my memory of twinkling blue water and darkness, plus Kim finding me wandering along the canal path.

Lois continued her confession. 'I only

realised you were back here when I spotted you at your gran's place. I'd been trying to find that damn blue jacket but you beat me to it. That's when I realised we'd have to move fast. One thing?' She faced Kim with a heartfelt plea. 'Could His Lordship have a proper burial, like? He's been down there alone far too long.'

'Yes, of course,' Kim replied sincerely.

After being checked by the ambulance team, I was taken back to Gran's home. It was over.

My family had been partly informed of the events of the day and it took quite a few biscuits and coffees before I could relate the whole sorry tale. Apparently, Rick had recovered his senses and was being kept in hospital overnight.

Darren Bruce was still out of it from prolonged exposure to the Dreamdust concoction. We assumed he must have come out of his hypnotic state for a short while in order to send his jacket through the waterways to seek help. It was a good thing he had. Otherwise we would never have realised where he was. His delighted family were with him.

Gran and I discussed why the injection had failed to subdue my free will. We could only speculate that it was an after-effect of previous exposure to both it and the Touch.

Exhausted mentally and physically, I actually dropped off to sleep on the settee. I vaguely recalled Amanda and Paul helping me to bed. That night I had visions of jewels and blue lights and long-dead Lords.

Then I dreamed of Rick by my side at a picnic. There were teddies sitting in a circle, with wolves and gooseberries all around as it poured with rain.

It was a good dream. In addition, I was now certain we could solve the riddle to discover where the treasure really was.

15

Amanda and Paul drove to the hospital the following morning. It was a two-fold visit; firstly, to see how Darren was recovering, then secondly to collect Rick.

Darren was apparently in reasonable health in spite of his month-long ordeal at Lois's beck and call. She had some fantastic idea that the valuables were secreted under water and needed a diver to check. The fact that they didn't have scuba divers at the time of the Reformation never seemed to have entered her mixed-up brain.

Darren had turned up at Nibberton Manor asking about the treasure. She'd discovered he was a diver so she used the Dreamdust on him, effectively kidnapping the poor man. Her plan was to let him go once the riches were found.

Darren's wife and children were by his bedside. Once Amanda introduced me, I was almost crushed by their hugs and thanks. Mr Bruce was groggy but slowly regaining his own free will.

Rick was dressed, sitting by his bed and impatient to leave, maintaining that he was perfectly fine. I decided to check.

'Rick. Give me a kiss.'

He stood to put his lips on mine. The kiss was still pathetic. Either he was still in his trace-like state a bit or, heaven forbid, his kiss was as good as I could ever expect.

Then he laughed.

'Got you going, Tammy. I might not have been able to make my own decisions in that underground place, but I remember what happened . . . every single bit.'

I was mortified for a moment, then grinned.

'So, Mr Detective. What are you really like?'

He took me in his arms to show me.

Amanda and Paul excused them-selves from the room after the first twenty seconds. Once our lips parted and I could breathe properly once more, Rick had to ask how that compared. I didn't have the heart to tell him that he was my first.

'Seven and a half. Maybe an eight,' I replied in my best not-impressed tone.

'Maybe you need more practice,' he joked.

Amanda appeared from the corridor.

'Come on, you two. We'd best get home. Kim will be waiting and there's still work to do.' She glanced at me.

Rick looked at me wide-eyed.

'You figured it out? I knew you could.'

'Not entirely, DS Turpin. But things are falling into place.'

* * *

Back at Gran's place, it was time for another brain-storming session. The

last one had been less than a spectacular success, yet I had hopes we could
break through the cryptic code that
Cyril had chosen to share with my
grandparents.

It was my belief that, having realised
that he'd inadvertently told Lois about
the riches, his slightly mixed-up mind
tried to make amends to the best friend
from his childhood . . . Gran.

In my ancestor's diary, I'd found a
reference to him moving the fortune so
that Armageddon Nibberton couldn't
get his greedy mitts on it.

I suspected that Cyril, as an adult,
was wont to revisit sites from his
childhood happy places. He'd discovered the final location of the treasure;
the place where Eugene Hathaway had
stashed the valuables. He hadn't trusted
Lois — though he did trust Gran to do
the right thing.

'Everyone ready?' I asked. We were
seated in Gran's lounge again — the
place where this bizarre adventure had
begun less than a week earlier.

Kim had brought and set up two overhead projectors and screens. One had the six clues written on acetate and displayed.

Hot drinks were distributed, as Gran maintained they relaxed the brain. I wasn't sure about that, but I did know I needed my custards. I returned from the kitchen clutching two packets; one for me, one for the rest of our think-tank.

'Tammy,' scolded Amanda. 'You're addicted to that rubbish. You'll end up looking like the Michelin Woman if you're not careful.'

'Gran says the custard helps combat the long-term effects of the Touch,' I said, being slightly disingenuous. Gran opened her eyes wide but didn't contradict my white lie.

'And they are only temporary. Shall we start? We need to think laterally . . . outside the obvious. I'm open to suggestions at any time.'

Our big Scooby-Doo gang watched as I wrote the key words up on the second projector.

Big, bad wolf, *Teddy's picnic,* *Gooseberries* and *Vervain* were the four headings I wrote on the acetate. It was just like being back in school.

'What I need are words or ideas associated with them.'

Gran kicked things off.

'Like I said, vervain is a common herb, though not so much hereabouts.' I wrote that up.

No one else volunteered anything.

'Big, bad wolf? Words connected with wolf, anyone?'

Paul spoke up. 'Werewolf, wolfram, wolfsbane, wolfing something down. Wolfram is the chemical name for tungsten, used in light bulbs. I am a chemist, after all.'

It was the longest utterance from him I'd ever heard. I wrote up his suggestions.

Rick suggested the Latin name for wolf, lupus.

'Loopy, that disease — lupus, loop the loop, loophole?'

Gran had been examining the list. 'Wolfsbane is another name for Arnica. I've only seen it in a few places in the Valley. There was vervain nearby.'

I thought about that. 'Big, bad wolf. If someone is bad, they're the bane of your life. Wolfsbane?'

From the expressions of my compatriots it made sense. They sat forward in their chairs eager to contribute if they could.

'What about Teddy and the picnic?' I asked Gran, aware it was well over sixty years ago.

'We had lots of picnics. There was no Teddy or Edward though. As for the gooseberries, we all collected them. Young Chris used to scoff them down by the handful.'

'Chris. What was his last name, Gran?'

'Goodness, child. Can you recall the name of a boy from sixty years ago?' She paused before concentrating her thoughts. 'Robin . . . Robinson. Chris Robinson. Happy now?'

312

I went over to give her a hug. 'Actually, Gran, I am. That's fantastic.'

It was Kim who saw the connection first among the others.

'Chris Robinson . . . Christopher Robin . . . Winnie the Pooh. His teddy bear.'

'His first book came out in 1926,' I said.

The timing fitted.

The others twigged straight away. Gran said, 'Actually Chris allus wore a jumper with Pooh Bear on it. His ma knitted it. Just remembered summat. Has anyone a map of the Valley?'

Kim produced one from her briefcase, turning on the main lights so we could gather around it.

Gran swapped her glasses, murmuring as she scanned the detailed map.

'There it is. Top of Beggar's Hill. There's wolfsbane and vervain there . . . and gooseberry bushes near an old cave. I'd forgot about that place. Chris got lost in there once. I remember 'cause we saw some biplanes flying overhead, them old Sopwith Elephants.'

'Camels, Mum. Not elephants,' Amanda chuckled.

'Anyway. We thought they were coming to search for Chris but they were simply doing aerobatics.'

'Like loop-the-loop?' Rick said.

Gran smiled. 'Exactly like loop-the-loop.'

We all took a moment to absorb the implications until Amanda summed it up in words.

'That's it then. It seems Eugene Hathaway's secret hiding place is no secret any longer. What do we do?'

'Well, I don't know about you,' Kim joked, 'but early retirement in the Bahamas sounds quite appealing.' We all stared at her in shock. 'Seriously though, we have to report it. Too many of us are aware of it now — plus blabbermouth Lois will be telling the world about the treasure in Arcana Valley. Our lives will be hell. We check it's true first, then get the Government involved. That's why Darren was here in the first place. Time to give the treasure back to the people.'

Amanda stood up, showing some distress.

'But unfortunately, you'll have to do it without me. All this excitement . . . I think Junior wants to be a part of it too.' She patted her tummy.

Paul rushed to her side. 'The baby's coming?'

Amanda nodded.

'Ambulance . . . blankets . . . hot water. Quick.' Paul began to panic.

'Not just now, lover-boy,' Amanda assured him. 'The contractions have only just begun.'

'There's a police car outside. No need for an ambulance. Go on, you two. I'll tell the driver.'

And just like that, all our lives changed forever.

16

There was no point concealing the treasure any longer. Once a secret is shared, it's a secret no longer.

A few months later, I'd moved to my new home in the Valley. Manchester seemed so tame by comparison, so I'd sold up and used some of the finder's fee I was given to buy Amanda's share of the house which Gran had once owned.

Actually, we'd all shared in the windfall from the Treasure Trove arrangement — even Rick and Kim.

There had been some dispute about that by the faceless bureaucrats in the government but, like the reversal of the decision to display the gold and jewellery in London, that problem had been smoothed over. It had been a joint effort searching out and finding the cache of riches in that cave, so we all deserved equal shares of the finder's fee.

'How's it going, Tammy?' Amanda called from the bathroom.

'Great. He's no trouble at all, are you, Jason?'

My nephew had made such a difference to my life. I really belonged to my family now.

Paul had been overseas again though he was taking a few days off to return to Hebden for the Grand Opening this afternoon. The Display Rooms and massive car parks had been completed in record time. The Thesaurus Crucis, or Treasure of the Cross Exhibition, would draw thousands of people to the area and the arrangement was that the profits from entry fees would be shared among local charities. I was one of the trustees.

With the aid of computers, I could work from anywhere I wanted and business was good. Amazing what a little publicity could do in the high finance field I was part of.

What was even better, we now had a postie delivering to the house.

As for Arcana Valley, it still had its secrets and mysteries, and it was my self-appointed role to investigate and protect them.

There was the strange creature I'd seen years ago in Misty River and recently in the Sea of Shadows. Also, the mystifying sound of ringing church bells from the end of the Valley where no roads, buildings or people existed.

What about the ruins of a medieval castle which only appeared on Sundays? Finally, why had the Romans called it Arcana or Secret Valley? Did they discover something, even back then?

'Hi, everyone. We're back,' Rick called out as he and Paul came through the front door of my building site of a home. I'd decided it was in dire need of modernisation.

Rick and I were enjoying life and romance together, free from the drama of those first few days with Lois, Kyle and Steve. As for me, I felt better than I ever had, learning about herbs and such from my clever Gran.

'We're in here,' I called back just as Amanda emerged looking absolutely stunning. I had to change into the smart satin three-piece I'd recently bought, then stick some lippy on — but, other than that, I was ready.

Rick and Paul had already changed into their suits, Paul at the airport where Rick had picked him up. I gave Rick a loving kiss. Life was good.

'What's that?' I asked, noting he was holding the mail in his hand. He must have collected it from the letterbox at the front gate.

Sensing that it contained something important, I flipped through the half dozen envelopes.

'Work . . . bill . . . work . . . work . . .' I paused, gazing at the one in my hand.

'What is it, babe?' Rick asked.

I showed it to him.

'Two Lady of the Lake stamps. Well, it can't be Cyril Andover. He's dead. And it can't be Lois or her crew. Prison has strict mail privileges. Shall I open it, Tammy?'

'No, Rick. It's addressed to me. As for the stamps it's probably a coincidence.'

Amanda put her hand on mine.

'Tammy. You don't believe in coincidences.'

She was right. I doubted there'd be any fingerprints, though I opened it carefully just in case. Gingerly I took out the single sheet, then opened it for all of us to see.

The coloured letters were cut from magazines and glued neatly to the page. It was chilling to read the message. It seemed my gentle life was going to change once more.

Tamara Arcana Jordan . . . Do you want to know a secret?

Other titles in the
Linford Romance Library:

KISS ME, KATE

Wendy Kremer

When Kate Parker begins work as the new secretary at a domestic head hunting company, the last thing she expects is to fall for her boss! Ryan Hayes, who runs the firm with his uncle, is deliciously appealing. But beautiful and elegant Louise seems to have a prior claim to him, and what man could resist her charms? Plus an old flame makes an appearance in Kate's life. Could she and Ryan have a future together — especially after Louise comes out with a shock announcement?